PENDRAGON: THE HAND OF GLORY

Book 2 of the Pendragon series.

Each book in the Pendragon series forms a complete story in itself.

London 1594: Nimue, daughter of the Queen's 'other Welsh wizard,' is entrusted by the Queen with a mission that only she, with her unique powers, can carry out. Her quest takes her into the Elizabethan Theatre of her father's friend Will Shakespeare, into the secret world of the cunning women, alchemists and dealers in magic. Her dreams lead her to the wild western coast of Ireland, to the great Cliffs of Moher. In serving her Queen and country as the youngest of the Pendragon wise men and women, Nimue arrests threatening evil and finds lasting happiness . . .

Books by Katrina Wright
in the Linford Romance Library:

FROM GREECE WITH LOVE
MASKED LOVE
WAIT UNTIL DARK
LOVE ON A DARK ISLAND
LOVE ON THE NILE
A DANGEROUS LOVE
SUSANNAH'S SECRET
SHADOW OF CLORINDA
THE SPY IN PETTICOATS
LOVE IN THE SPOTLIGHT
SECRET OF THE SNOWS

PENDRAGON:
THE WIZARD'S DAUGHTER BOOK 1

KATRINA WRIGHT

PENDRAGON 2:
THE HAND
OF GLORY

Complete and Unabridged

LINFORD
Leicester

First published in Great Britain in 1999

First Linford Edition
published 2000

British Library CIP Data

Wright, Katrina
    Pendragon: the hand of glory.—Large print ed.—
Linford romance library
1. Love stories
2. Large type books
I. Title
823.9'14 [F]

ISBN 0–7089–5735–8

Published by
F. A. Thorpe (Publishing)
Anstey, Leicestershire

Set by Words & Graphics Ltd.
Anstey, Leicestershire
Printed and bound in Great Britain by
T. J. International Ltd., Padstow, Cornwall

This book is printed on acid-free paper

To my friend Mary Lehane in Lahinch, Co. Clare, and her family, Anna, Frank, Maura and Sarah. And to Agnes O'Brien and all my other friends in Ireland.

1

Like all journeys, the long ride had ended at last, here in the small, richly-appointed antechamber in the royal palace of Greenwich.

Nimue was very tired after unaccustomed days in the saddle, and the candles in their silver sconces seemed to be flickering in and out of her vision, in shapes that changed disconcertingly. In her heightened, exhausted state, she was aware of some sort of presence in the room, something formless that nevertheless made her shiver suddenly and pull her cloak about her. It was weariness, she told herself, and turned her head as Arabella Nevile came, soft-footed in her velvet shoes, from the apartment beyond.

'Her Grace has been waiting for you,' the Queen's privy lady told Nimue, with no preliminaries. 'Come.'

And, travel-stiff with her skirts still splashed from the February roads, her riding hood pulled back to reveal the soft dark curls that clustered close round her head like the petals of the oriental flower they called chrysanthemum, Nimue moved as though in a dream to follow her through the door that was discreetly concealed behind the arras, into the presence of Elizabeth of England.

She had seen the Queen before, many times but from a distance, as a glittering, regal icon, when she and her father had been living in the small house near London Bridge, and it had seemed that things would never change. One never knew how precious were the everydays one took for granted until they were not there. Was it only a year — no, far less than that — since Gereint Gwynne had died, coughing painfully and shrunken on his narrow bed, and his daughter had followed his wishes and gone with Gilbert Stoneyathe and his sister Mary to the wilds of North Wales?

It seemed no more than the memory of an old tale to her now, as she found herself in the Queen's presence, dipping to the ground in a deep curtsey. It was true she had been born in Wales, but she could not remember that, so what had she, who had lived all her life in London, to do with that mysterious, legendary country of princes and poets? It was as though she had never left the city that was the heart of England, never encountered the rider of that white horse of myth and magic, never lived the enchanted night of Christmas when, in the dimness of the shrine of St Mary beside the Elwy, she and the wizard Merlin Pendragon, who had been her dear, scarred lord of dark and light, had been married by the hermit — .

A voice broke in on her thoughts, cool and commanding.

'Mistress Gwynne.'

And, unable to help herself, Nimue looked up into the face of the Queen with all her pain naked in her green-gold eyes.

'Your Grace, I am Mistress Gwynne no longer. I have lived a lifetime since my father died and I went with Stoneyathe to Wales. I have the honour now to be your obedient servant to command, Mistress Nimue Pendragon, the wife to Pendragon of Pendragon tower. Alas, no longer his wife but his widow, though never his in very truth.'

The Queen's eyes, which sometimes looked so dark as to be almost black, were in the light of the candles the colour of a peculiarly precious Spanish sherry wine. Her brows, thinly drawn, lifted at the young woman's words.

'Indeed. Yet there are matters of greater moment that I must discuss with you, madam,' she said sharply, so that Nimue was shaken out of herself. Her breath came quickly, as though the Queen had doused her beneath the pump in icy water. What did it matter to Elizabeth, or indeed to

4

anyone, the wonder and the sorrow that had happened to her? The Queen had the kingdom upon her conscience, all the souls of the teeming multitudes who were her subjects.

She seemed to hear her father's voice, as he had spoken many times when he was alive, lightly, but with underlying deep seriousness.

'The strong cannot afford to weep, to mourn. That indulgence is for the weak, who have not yet learned that no spirit is given a burden it cannot carry.'

Nimue thought she had never really understood before the meaning of those words. Still sunk in her curtsey, she lifted her head and stiffened her back.

'Your Grace will pardon my weariness,' she said quietly. 'I have been riding many days to come in response to your summons. Madam, how can I serve you?'

Elizabeth smiled suddenly, and the smile transformed her pale face, which Nimue saw now was heavily powdered, and beneath the mask of powder, was drawn and old. But her eyes were very alive.

'Rise, mistress,' she ordered, and turned. 'Arabella, where is the wine? This child is pinched and perishing.'

She waved towards a richly tapestried stool, and thankfully, Nimue sank onto it, taking the cup Arabella handed to her and sipping the liquid within. The Queen's voice spoke on, as though it came from a far distance, or out of a mist.

'We let you go when your father died, thinking you were of no account, since it was expedient to do so. But we have not forgotten that you are your father's daughter. My other Welsh wizard, your father, gave me faithful counsel and always spoke me true. I mourn his loss, do not believe otherwise, but a king must not be seen to value any save as servants of the state.'

She paused, and Nimue, warmed now by the wine and the heat of the fire that burned in the room, smelling of herbs and other fugitive woody scents, waited. She sensed that Elizabeth had been speaking absently, almost carelessly, and was only now about to voice her true concerns.

'Do you know ought of the Hand, mistress?'

The question was unexpected, yet when it came, Nimue felt it as inevitable as the shiver that touched her again, as it had done before in the antechamber. She looked directly into the Queen's hooded eyes.

'I do not know of it, Your Grace, yet I can sense its presence. It bodes ill.' She paused, while Elizabeth, a shrewd diplomat, waited.

'There is darkness,' Nimue said at last, groping through layers of intuition. 'I can see no more. Some powerful force — dark magic, my father would have called it, a greed that feeds on evil and on which evil is allowed to feed — blocks the vision.'

Elizabeth's face was expressionless,

but her voice was sharp with something like satisfaction.

'So we have been told. So our other informants have told us. It hangs weightily upon us, this information. For, mistress, there has always been greed for power, and there have always been those who would turn to evil. Your father knew of this and he was strong in the right. Stronger than any other.'

Nimue felt sudden tears prick behind her eyes at this unexpected tribute. Elizabeth leaned across and took the girl's chin in her long, white fingers, tilting up her face, her eyes searching.

'If your father had been here,' she said. 'If he had been here, my other Welsh wizard — . But he is not, only his daughter. You have the look of him, child, that light of other wisdom in your face. I have no need of wizards for the temporal, I can deal with traitors. And my bishops will do the pleading with the Almighty. But this is different. They have all told me, John Dee and the rest, that this is from a darker world, this — Hand.'

Nimue felt the piercing eyes command her.

'They are known, my wizards and cunning women,' the Queen stated matter of factly. 'But you, scarcely a woman, a child who lived innocent of the dark with your father, you are of no account to any, your powers are unproven. Only you can act for us, seeming to threaten no-one, unsuspected. You will seek out the source of this evil, and as you are your father's daughter, so you will do whatever is necessary for all of us to bring about its defeat.'

★ ★ ★

She would have to act a role, play a part, Burleigh told her when she left the Queen's presence and Arabella conducted her to another room, more spare and Spartan, where he was sitting at a table with papers before him. He was an old man, in his seventies, and

9

ailing, but his face was lean and controlled, the face of an ascetic, his eyes ruthless with disinterested detachment. Nimue was aware, as his first glance lifted towards her, that he did not approve of Elizabeth's decision to place such a heavy responsibility in the hands of a young woman with no experience of such matters. But he was the Queen's closest adviser and he respected her shrewdness and political flair. He would carry out his instructions and provide Nimue with all the information and assistance he could.

Composedly she seated herself on the chair that was placed for her, while Arabella slipped from the room to return to her mistress. The hour was very late and the Queen, who had been famed for her ability to dance the night away and yet be up with the dawn at private counsel before leading her courtiers in the hunt, was an old and tired woman who must be attended on in her bedchamber. In emotionless tones, Burleigh proceeded to outline the situation while Nimue listened.

It had come to his attention, he said, from sources he had no reason to doubt, though they were to be found in the stews and bear gardens and the teeming underworld of Southwark, that some movement, some plot or revolution, some kind of revolt or rebellion, was in existence, gathering force, threatening the very peace of the kingdom. It was whispered of as the Hand — sometimes the Hand of Glory — and the whispers were invariably accompanied by a lifted arm as the informer crossed himself or touched the amulet that hung greasily about his neck to ward off evil.

'Plots,' Burleigh said drily, 'are always with us, mistress, as are rumours of plots. The broadsheets are even now calling for the death of the traitor Dr Lopez, who for thirty years has lived in the highest esteem of the Queen and has attended her person. What do we find?' He paused briefly. 'This estimable doctor, the physician to half the court, has been serving Spain it seems, though I am not convinced. But he will die, there is no doubt, sentence is already passed — when the person of the Queen's Majesty is at risk, we can take no chances.'

★ ★ ★

And so at last she reached the true ending of her journey — the journey that had begun at her father's death bed, and taken her to the wild country in the west where she had stood with Pendragon in the tiny chapel of St Mary and sworn her vows with him on the hilt of his sword. And then, in a glory of love and laughter, drunk sops in wine for her wedding breakfast in the hermit's cell before they mounted their horses and disappeared again into the snowy dawn.

There was a small house on the bank of the Thames, with an apple tree and a herb bed and a little dovecote where the white doves cooed and shimmered in the softly falling rain. Nimue walked in the garden on the morning following her arrival, her cloak wrapped round her. It was peaceful and she was glad, for she needed time to think. Too much had happened in too short a time.

The rain was soft as mist on her hair, and the air was sweet with the scents of growing things stirring in the February earth. She stood at the water-steps, where the garden ended at the river's edge, and looked across the shining expanse of the Thames. Behind her lay the dark glitter of the city. London, where her father had lived exiled from his native Wales and she had grown up. Now she need never leave it again, for she was a woman of property. All this — she turned her head wonderingly to look at the black and white gable of the little house, its casements bright and polished — was hers, the gift of the Queen of England. Hers in perpetuity, as her father's daughter, who would continue to serve the Crown as Gereint Gwynne had done, counselling and advising with her special powers of clear sight and true wisdom. Elizabeth had promised her this.

It had seemed too wonderful to be true, that having returned alone, parted from the husband and the future life that had promised so much, Nimue should be given a house of her own, a jointure that would make her independent for the rest of her life. And a standing, a status in society. A young woman — a widow — of position now, not only the wizard's daughter but a lady in her own right, with the dignity of grief on her shoulders like a mantle. No longer the child who had ridden trustingly into the west believing in the promise of destiny, but the widowed Mistress Pendragon, soberly bereaved and settling into the quiet life of a respectable gentlewoman.

Burleigh had explained in emotionless tones, when she expressed her amazement at the Queen's gift, that it was necessary if for no other reason than that Nimue should be placed in a position of unimpeachable respectability for her to begin her investigations into the mysterious and secretive activities of the Hand.

'Whoever is responsible, they will undoubtedly have knowledge of your father and of his daughter,' he said. 'There is deep magic here, and such magicians know their own kind. They will know also the cunning men and women, I have no doubt, and have taken their measure. You are one of them, by your birth and your father's instruction, but as yet unproven, untried.'

He gave a mirthless smile. Nimue waited.

'It is Her Grace's wish that you do not take lodgings in some alehouse, however reputable. In your own establishment I can see that you are protected — so far as it is possible.'

'The Queen is generous,' Nimue said impulsively, and Burleigh looked at her with his remote eyes.

'Plotters and traitors are no respecters of person, Mistress Pendragon. There may be very real danger, it is vital you realise that if you are found to be meddling in the affairs of traitors, rebels or revolutionaries and reporting to me — far less acting independently against them for the state — you might not survive. Though naturally, Her Majesty has instructed me to take all possible steps to make sure that you do not come to harm, she is a realist. In the event of your decease, by whatever means, within the year, your property will revert back to the Crown.'

Nimue stared at him, wanting suddenly to dissolve into laughter, which she recognised as born of weariness and the strangeness of the situation in which she found herself. When the Queen had told her of the task she was to undertake, she had quietly accepted that she was being asked to risk not only her life but what was even more precious, her soul. It was not something to be taken lightly. Black magicians, her father had said on the few occasions he had spoken of such matters, were not to be feared for their power, but for their intent to use evil for their own ends.

'It is not the evil one who is the enemy, Nimue,' he had told her, his brows drawn together and his eyes clouded. 'It is the greed and the selfishness which can make a man welcome evil into his heart and conspire with the dark against his fellows. The black magician is not strong, he is weak, yet never underestimate weakness. The fear that rides side by side with weakness is the real enemy.'

The prospect before her was of frightening magnitude, and the fact that it was she, young and untried, who had been summoned to carry it through — the fact that the Queen had said bluntly that she believed the daughter of her 'other Welsh wizard' must possess the power and the integrity that would be needed to oppose any dark plot, was humbling. All the same, the single-minded practicality of the Queen lifted her tired spirits and brought a spark of irrepressible amusement to her eyes. Casting her gaze down in case Burleigh should mistake the humour for irresponsibility, she managed to reply composedly: 'I am well aware of the danger if I should fail, sir. But both my father and my husband served the cause of the truth, the light. I will do so to the best of my ability, and I am grateful to the Queen for providing a place where I may do it in some comfort and privacy. But if it is my fate to die in my endeavours, I have,' she said in a tone as disinterested as his own, 'no-one to inherit the Queen's gift from me. Her Majesty makes provision for everything.'

★ ★ ★

Standing beside the fretted waters of the Thames in the rain, she turned suddenly as there was a voice behind her, a deep voice that spoke her name. She saw Huw, the dark-skinned mute who had been her husband's faithful servant and companion, attempting to bar the way to another figure in a red cloak. Beneath the unruly hair, the newcomer's eyes laughed and mocked at her, eyes that seemed to transport her back to the evenings beside the hearth in the old days in the house near London Bridge.

'Will, how did you know I was here?' she cried, her hand going to her throat, her feelings rising as though they would overwhelm her. 'You may let him pass, Huw, he is my oldest friend, my father's and mine. Will Shakespeare, the actor. Oh, Will — I thought I would never see you again. Oh, Will, but you are welcome.'

He smiled now, the breeze from the river tousling his dark hair, the rain silvering his mobile actor's face. He was solid and very masculine, and she was suddenly confused, extremely conscious of his physical closeness, remembering their last meeting, the last time she had seen him on the wintry shore of the estuary of the Dee below the dark bulk of Flint Castle. She had sent him away from her, refusing his protestations of love. But Will had no mean spirit and he made no attempt to take advantage of her pleasure at seeing him or her newly vulnerable state. His eyes were clear and warm, with no passion to distress her or distract from their old friendship. He was a link with the past, with her father, and she felt nothing but a lifting of her heart as he took both her hands in his.

'Oh, the city never sleeps, all is known to the watchmen,' he grinned. 'I came as soon as I heard. No wizardry now, you are a woman of property then, the Queen remembered your father.' His voice was uncharacteristically gruff, for Gereint Gwynne had been close to him, more than just a friend, a mentor and guide, a companion of the soul.

'Yes,' Nimue answered simply. She was wondering what sort of tales had been spread — by Burleigh himself, perhaps? — about her return to London. If Will had heard them, so would others know of her whereabouts and circumstances.

Will was looking out across the river, dark in the rain.

'You left him, then,' he said, as though it mattered little to him. 'That man, Pendragon, the one who had taken your imagination? He was not the man you thought, not worthy of you. Was that how it was, girl?'

'Oh, Will,' she said, and her breath caught in her throat. She turned away herself. She bit her lip, mindful that she had new responsibilities now, such as she had never dreamed she would have to carry. She was responsible not only to the Queen and to Burleigh but to all the humbler people, the ordinary everyday men and women who were even now going about their business,

21

unaware, throughout the length and breadth of the country. Whatever she did, she must be mindful that it might contribute to their peace, or lack of it.

She hesitated. Will Shakespeare loved her, she knew that, he loved her as a man loved the dream that haunted his sleep and walked with him in his inner strivings. She was his Dark Lady who led him through the wilderness of his creative thoughts, the muse who guided his pen when he tried to capture his inspiration in lines of poetry or the words of a play.

But how far should she trust him? Would it be fair to him to lean on his feelings for her and use him for support? He had a wife and a family, to whom he owed his first loyalties. And he had his profession, a way to make for himself in the theatre.

After a moment, she turned back to him.

'Will, among the rumours of the city, the watchmen's talk, have you heard

mention of the Hand?' she
Hand of Glory?'

He looked at her with
for a long moment, his
Then he said, low and

'What is this, girl? Who has
gabbing to you?'

She knew then that she must keep
nothing from him. Secrecy and deceit,
her father's voice seemed to be urging
her, bred only secrecy and deceit. She
laid her fingers on the damp velvet of
Will's sleeve.

'Let us go in, and Huw shall bring
us some refreshment, and I will tell
you all.'

★ ★ ★

Within, there was fire and cheer, and
they sat in the little parlour. Nimue
leaned forward to warm her hands at
the blaze. She had become more chilled
than she had realised out in the rain.

'I married him, Will,' she said,
without looking at him. 'I married my

rd, Pendragon. And I have lost
I — do not want to speak of it, but
u must know that I am a widow now.
t was a time of violence and terror and
I will never forget it — nor forget him
— though it is best forgotten. But on
that night he perished in the flames, the
Queen sent for me and I am here only
to serve her. I have been instructed to
seek out something — someone — that
is talked of as the Hand. Do you know
ought of it?'

Shakespeare was silent. His profile
was shadowed, the pale light from the
window caught the gleam of the single
gold ring in his ear. After a moment,
Nimue turned to him questioningly.

'What is it, Will?'

'You are different, girl,' he said in
a low voice. 'You have changed. I
want to protect you, warn you, for
your father's sake as well as for your
own, and yet, this time, I do not dare
to presume.'

'Warn me?' she queried.

'You speak of the Hand,' he said,

and she sensed rather than saw that he made an effort to still himself from making some gesture born of superstition, some gesture of self-defence, protection against the evil eye, the evil one. The awareness chilled her more than anything else that had been said about the Hand.

'What is it, Will?' she demanded again, straight. 'You are afraid of nothing, yet this troubles you. You need not worry to tell me, the Queen sent for me to seek it out and confront it.' Seeing the leaping of concern in his eyes, she spread her hands and shrugged slightly.

'Oh, Will, you have heard my father say over and over that it is confusion and ignorance that breeds fear. When you know your enemy, then you can fight. Whatever this thing is, I must face it. My father would have served the Queen in this matter, but she has appointed me in his place and honoured me by giving me her confidence and trust. And Will, I married into these

25

duties also. I can never forget that I am a Pendragon now. My husband and his forbears served kings and princes with counsel and wisdom, since the time of Arthur. I have been given my powers for a reason, to use them for good. I will not be a coward, I know this is dangerous but that is why the Queen sent for me. She needed a white magician to fight the dark.'

Will regarded her quizzically, almost in fear.

'I am a plain man,' he said after a moment. 'I know the tricks of the theatre, girl, where lightning can strike from heaven, and the world can be encompassed in a wooden O. But the Hand — .' Again, there was that involuntary movement of his arm, quickly repressed. The medal of Genesius of Rome, protector of tumblers, mountebanks and players, gleamed at his throat, and Nimue knew he had been going to touch it.

'Tell me, Will,' she said steadily.

'And after all, I can tell you little,'

he said, troubled. 'There have been omens, portents, they say, and the plague still stalks the city. You know, since your father died of it. The theatres stand idle, we are forbidden to hold public gatherings for plays because of the danger of contagion.' He played with the tassel on his sleeve, whistling through his teeth. 'These are the warnings of the Hand, some whisper. I would not disturb you with this talk, girl, for I do not believe in a jealous God. I am a simple man, my faith is likewise simple — .'

'I know,' Nimue said involuntarily. 'It shines from you, Will. It has always done so. You do not have to explain.'

He half-laughed, his eyes mocking her.

'Your father is in you now, girl. You have come back a woman too wise for me.'

Nimue sighed, looking to where the rain misted the green branches of ivy that shadowed the casement.

'I will need all the wisdom I can

summon,' she said. 'But I am still the girl you knew, Will. I may appear different, but that is the illusion like your stage tricks.'

He covered her hand suddenly with his own, and she could feel the warmth of his fingers. There was a silence and a peace between them, that of comrades, of allies and friends. Her sorrow and need had succeeded in bringing them closer than all his romantic passion.

'There are rumours, painted and full of tongues,' he said at length. 'If you were to come with me to the taverns where the players meet, you might hear more. And I could watch over you. All of London knows I was your father's friend, what more natural than that I should seek to extend my protection over you now that he is dead and you are alone?'

'True,' Nimue agreed thoughtfully. She realised she would have to seek out the rumours, the gossip that was spread in secret. Burleigh had warned her that she would have to pretend to interest herself in the magical activities that were whispered abroad.

'You have inherited your father's powers, but who knows but that your nature is not for earthly and temporal rather than the things of the spirit?' the statesman had said, shrugging. 'If it is known you are living in the city — and the widow of a wizard of fearsome reputation — the Pendragons are so regarded by the country people I understand — it is likely that you will be contacted. Whoever is reponsible may seek you out to form some sort of an alliance with you.'

Nimue, considering, had thought it was sound reasoning. She would have to hold herself ready for whatever came, and be prepared to play her part skilfully. Now she turned to Will, serious-faced.

'I can trust you, Will. You are the only person who knows of my true purpose except of course for Huw and Math. My husband's faithful companion, and his apprentice — Huw you have met and Math you will meet. They have come with me from my husband's country and are loyal to me to the death. They will protect me, but I will be guided by you. It is in the taverns that the Hand is whispered?'

'All gossip starts in the taverns,' Will said, and she nodded.

'Then I will go to the taverns. I will come with you and drink and listen. I have some property now, as well as my father's reputation for magic. I might be a woman of greed and ambition and lust for power, who knows — .'

He snapped his lean fingers, incredulous.

'You?'

'Others do not know me,' she argued. 'If there is something dark afoot they will not leave me untested. They will find whether I am for the dark or against it. Evil magic cannot be satisfied to let well alone. So I will come with you — and make it easy for them to find me.'

2

The playhouse looked draggled and dismal, but it was not so much because the rain was falling out of a grey and lowering sky, it was because there was nothing as miserable as a theatre that was standing empty — and the London theatres had been idle now for nearly two years.

Cuthbert Burbage, the elder son of the proprietor of The Theatre, was intense and overly dramatic as he propounded to Nimue his theory that the soul needed theatre as the body needed air to breathe and food to eat. But since the plague had hit the city, the Puritans and the killjoys had had their way and the Privy Council had forbidden all plays, baitings and assemblies except for preachings, leaving the players to scratch a living as best they could while the banners and bravery of the stage drooped silent in the empty playhouses.

Nimue listened sympathetically, though she found it difficult not to smile at Cuthbert's earnest white face, streaming with rain, and his cheese-like chin lowering beneath his thatch of thick tow hair. Cuthbert was no actor — it was his brother Richard who, as Will had informed her on their way to the theatre, was the genius of their company. He could hold audiences spellbound with his voice and presence. Not like Edward Alleyn, at the Rose, who relied on ravings and stampings in the character of Tamburlaine and other such tragic heroes to stir the lower sorts in the standings to shrieks of frenzied delight.

Will had spoken diffidently of his inmost preoccupations regarding his work to Nimue, since he told her frankly that his wife Anne was not of a mind to appreciate such conversation, being a practical woman with her cares for her children and their everyday doings. Alleyn's kind of acting was not for him nor his plays, he said, he preferred subtlety.

Nimue had been received at The Theatre as an honoured visitor and conducted by Cuthbert Burbage over the stage, the tiring house, the balcony. She was currently viewing the rows of galleries where the audiences were accommodated to watch the play, now gloomy indeed in the streaming rain, but her face beneath her hood was bright and interested.

Will had made the suggestion that if she wanted to attract the attention of any who might desire to sound her out, as a woman of property now, and perhaps some affluence (it was all to the good, he commented briefly with a negligent wave of his hand, that no-one in London knew much about Pendragon, or what sort of estate he might have left to his young widow) she might feign a desire for power within the world of acting. This had always been the prerogative of men, of the nobles, many of whom possessed their own companies of players, but it might serve Nimue's purpose to have it hinted abroad that she too, as a woman of wealth, was willing to be approached as a possible patroness of the arts — or of any other ventures that might interest her.

'Then in such a role, you would be able to go where you liked about the city,' he suggested.

It was a good plan, Nimue thought as she considered it. Simple, yet under his watchful glance and as a businesswoman with the protective escort of Huw and Math, she could move freely without stirring up suspicion or attracting the wrong sort of attention among the colourful gatherings of painters, eccentrics, gamesters, actors, poets and aspiring writers — even rogues and women of the streets — though no lady would normally have kept such company.

'But it is known you are Gereint

Gwynne's daughter, and when did he ever bow to convention?' Will had shrugged.

Nimue nodded soberly.

'Yes, it will then appear to observers that I am an unknown quantity, that I might well be interested — and influential, Will — in all sorts of dubious undertakings.'

And so here she was, standing in the company of some of Will's fellow actors in the empty playhouse in the rain. But she was genuinely interested in Cuthbert Burbage's earnest commentary on the theatre that was his empire. She had been to the playhouse many times, of course, with her father, but females formed no part of the ritualised world of the stage and no lady would lower herself to perform in public, however excellent a dancer or however sweet-voiced she might be in private.

Will's fellow actors, who had met Nimue at the empty playhouse, were much impressed by her youth and beauty as well as her poise. Cuthbert

Burbage chattered boyishly of their hopes — the hopes of the whole company — that the coming summer and the hopeful lifting of the plague restrictions would mark a fresh start for all of them after the last two years, perhaps with a new patron. He did not actually speak the word 'patroness' but it hung hopefully in the air and Nimue felt a sudden qualm at her masquerade. For she had no resources, in truth, to patronise anyone, her day to day expenses were being met from the Queen's modest gift accompanying the present of her house.

'You must live as befits a supposed woman of wealth,' Burleigh had told her, dismissing her surprise and expressions of thanks for the Queen's allowance brusquely. 'No doubt later, when the task is accomplished, Her Grace will wish to speak further concerning your settlement. I understand your — ah — husband left property in Wales.'

Nimue thought of the sight that would be stamped upon her mind for ever, the dark bulk of Pendragon tower burning, the flames roaring up into the night sky. She made an effort to erase the image and to reply composedly.

'Yes, sir, land and — .' Then the recollection of the gold, the presence somewhere on Pendragon land of that most precious of metals, the promise of which had driven Gilbert Stoneyathe to murder and had threatened her own safety, the gold that had been the cause of the crisis which had exploded upon them all on the night of the fire, came back to her. She hesitated, lost for a moment in her thoughts.

It had been Pendragon's old friend the Druid Owain ab Owain, stained with his years of working with metals in the wilderness of Halkyn Mountain, who had sent her from the scene of the fire, urgently bidden her ride at the Queen's summons, and leave all in his hands. He had promised her that he would take care of her interests and she had been too stricken, too lost in her grief, to do anything but obey him. But now, sanity had returned to her, and an awareness of her responsibilities. As Burleigh watched impassively she was silent for long moments, then she said slowly:

'There is much I must consider, sir. And perhaps, seek advice. Her Grace has been most generous, and I owe her more than I can ever repay. Yet, when I am able, I must seek advice — I have left tangled affairs behind me.'

Burleigh's brows, thick and white, shifted. His face was disinterested.

'In time, in time mistress,' he said dismissively. 'The task in hand will require all your attentions at present. The Queen has placed her confidence in you, more than I personally would have thought advisable.'

Nimue's head went up at his tone.

'I will not neglect the task for my own affairs, sir.'

He had given the briefest of shrugs, almost insulting in his disregard, and proceeded to turn the conversation to the details of the image she must create. In accordance with this part she played, Cuthbert Burbage was now eying her hopefully and talking about plans for the autumn. It went against her natural honesty to mislead him over her financial situation, but when they departed the playhouse for the tavern where the actors were accustomed to congregate to exchange news and gossip, and she said as much to Will, he snapped his fingers at her serious face.

'Don't fret for the Burbages, girl. They will never be poor men.' He flashed her his sudden mocking, self-deprecating grin. 'Is not the name of William Shakespeare enough to ensure the fortune of our company?'

Nimue smiled back, but said nothing. She had begun to realise now how he doubted himself, and how despite his bravado he thirsted for approval. All the actors who were with them had the same childlike quality about them, even the greybeard Benjamin Ashe. They could not live without attention, they hungered to be loved.

She looked about her with interest as they left the muddy street for the dim confines of the tavern, stepping beneath the low lintel with its carvings below the swinging inn sign. The room was tiny and crowded, resounding with much talk but at the same time curiously intimate, and cosily warmed by two roaring fires. A tall thin figure somewhat resembling a Maypole loomed out of the smoke that curled from long tobacco pipes and the smells of food roasting and fresh brewed ale, and planted itself in front of Will.

'Shame upon you! It is not enough that your poor, longsuffering wife awaits you in vain! Would you also risk perdition for consorting with pretty drabs?' reproved an unexpectedly high, but carrying voice, and Will, at Nimue's elbow, turned sharply to the speaker.

'Jealous, Ardua? Name of the blood, if I was a true gentleman I would challenge you hotly in defence of

Mistress Pendragon's honour — yet she will pardon me, for no gentleman would strike a female, even when she speaks out of sourness and has forsworn her sex.' To Nimue, he added, with a brief gesture of introduction: 'Madam, this beanpole of a gentleman is none other than the Lady Ardua, who plots tirelessly to save all our souls, whether we will be saved or no. She will, I am sure, be anxious to amend her unfortunate remark, lest she sully a good and honest name. Of your charity, you will pardon her light speech.'

He was angry, Nimue thought, but she herself was more amused by the creature's impertinence. She looked back with interest as a piercing gaze was bent upon her through the murk of the room. The Lady Ardua must have been sixty if she was a day. She was taller than any man present, and her scrawny flatness was accentuated by her man's attire of jerkin and hose in rusty black fustian trimmed with black mildewed velvet. Her legs disappeared as crookedly as those of a spider into tight-fitting boots of shabby leather and she was, even to the most charitably disposed observer, a startlingly grotesque figure.

As Nimue stared up into the brown weather-beaten face, however, she was struck by the strange woman's eyes, which were the colour of faded pansies, dark with arcane knowledge. Above them, sparse hair stuck out from her head in an untidy crop like bristly stubble, which had been clumsily dyed in an effort to hide the grey. The result was a streaky patchwork effect of black, grey and white, like a brindled cat.

Those disturbing eyes surveyed Nimue for a moment before Lady Ardua spoke. Then she said severely:

'Mistress Pendragon! Ha! I mistake me, it seems madam.' She sketched a bow. 'Your servant. But the ignorant and the foolish must be guided. You can do no good even to a pious reputation if you will haunt the stews like any light female. And in company with mountebanks — .'

'Players, not mountebanks, woman. We are thespians in a great tradition,' growled the elderly Benjamin Ashe, while the two pretty young men who played the female parts nudged each other and tossed their heads and tittered aloud, rolling their eyes.

Lady Ardua, with magnificent savoir faire, ignored them and renewed her attack on Will.

'Have you no thought for the sanctity of marriage?' she continued, her voice trumpeting into every corner of the room. She turned majestically upon Nimue. 'And you, madam, what is your husband about, to countenance your gadding? Too old and gouty to think of aught but taking his ease before the fire, no doubt, and too soft to administer the proper beatings that would keep you docile. But take warning, even the most equable disposition can be enflamed if you push it too far.'

Nimue's breath went out in an involuntary gasp, and she almost laughed

43

aloud. It was not possible to take such an outrageous attack seriously, the Lady Ardua was as ridiculous a character as any Will Shakespeare might create in his plays — and her heart twisted as she thought how her husband would have reacted if he had heard. With what dry irony, what droll delight he would have savoured the jest. But, biting her lip to preserve her gravity, she veiled her eyes before responding:

'You mean well, I am sure, ma'am, but I have known Mister Shakespeare for many years as one of my late father's dearest friends. Now that I am, alas, alone in the world I regard him even more fondly as in loco parentis.'

Ignoring Will's smothered snort of quick amusement beside her, she added quietly. 'And though I own I might well be the better for a beating or two from my husband, he is alas no longer on this earth to provide them. I am a widow.'

But the Lady Ardua never faltered.

'Circumstances are no excuse for laxity,' she pronounced severely. 'You are nevertheless still very young I observe, mistress, and could at any time fall a prey to the temptations that lurk within such establishments as this one. Go home, say your prayers and look for another husband to guide you.'

'A second challenge Ardua,' Will reprimanded and he was no longer amused. 'Did you never learn, in all your wise preaching, that each must find salvation in his own way?'

'The Counsellor never gives up hope,' the Lady Ardua announced vigorously, and Will turned to mumble into his cup of ale.

'More's the pity.'

His irritation was on her behalf, Nimue knew, and she smiled to show him that she was not angry or hurt. In return, he lifted his eyes in a gesture of exasperation, and shrugged. With no further word or nod, the Lady Ardua moved away.

'Who is she?' Nimue asked, intrigued, and Will shrugged again.

'God knows. She appeared for the first time here in the taverns at the Yule festivities, poking her beaky nose unwanted into all our affairs as you heard and supposedly after mending our ways for us. The eccentric dependent of some noble house, I would imagine, for she has money in spite of those rustic looks.' At Nimue's further glance of interest, he rolled his eyes melodramatically. 'Well, her religion, whatever it is, has brought her a man too. She lodges at the house of a kinswoman of one of our company — and for the last few weeks has shared a parlour with the Counsellor she mentioned. But he brings her no joy, you can be sure of that. He is another who would put a stop to all the pleasures that make life worth living, and for all that he is so pious, he has a boldness about him.' He paused, then added, in a tone that brought Nimue's head sharply up. 'Some have begun to call him the Holy Devil.'

But then, as Will could not remain uncharitable for long, his expression cleared. 'Oh, they are harmless enough. Irritants merely, like flies.'

'Are they Puritans?' Nimue queried, trying to peer through the bodies of the tavern customers in the smoky room to the corner where the Lady Ardua could be glimpsed in earnest conversation with another figure.

'Puritans? Say nihilists, rather,' growled Benjamin Ash feelingly and the others laughed.

Nimue, thoughtfully lingering, saw as the crowd in the room shifted, that the Lady Ardua's companion was a man who wore a dark cloak with a plain black hat. It was difficult to make out his age, for his face was all but obscured by straight black hair to his shoulders, and a thick black beard. He looked up suddenly as though aware of her gaze, straight towards her but without haste, deliberately. His eyes, deeply black and burning as coals, caught hers. He lifted his hand and made the sign of the cross, and Nimue turned away strangely breathless, her colour heightening.

It had been as direct as a gauntlet thrown down, that look. It had been a challenge, a threat. She did not need to call on her intuitive powers. Every nerve in her body was thrumming with the awareness that whoever, whatever he might be, this was a dangerous man.

★ ★ ★

In the quietness of her own rooms, alone, with the waters of the Thames running beneath the sharp rods of rain below the water steps and the fire Huw had kindled crackling cheerfully on her own hearth, Nimue sat in the gathering dark. She had the ring of heavy silver set with its translucent stone that glowed emptily, holding the mysteriousness of no colour within its depths, on her finger. The moonstone that Pendragon had given her was, together with her father's great crystal, her most precious possession and she was grateful of its weight on her hand tonight, feeling the coolness of the jewel calming and clearing her mind.

The encounter, brief though it had been, with the man in the black cloak in the tavern — and she wondered uneasily what sort of 'counsel' he was accustomed to giving to those who might consult him — had disturbed her. She could not yet fathom the depth or the nature of his power, but power she knew intuitively was there. But had it been only coincidence that, seeking some clue as to the existence of a movement filled with dark magic that threatened the kingdom, she should so soon encounter a man who possessed the kind of power that she suspected could challenge her own belief in the power of the light?

Again, as so often when she needed guidance, she seemed to hear her father's voice, counselling, warning.

'In this life there are no coincidences, Nimue.'

She thought back to what Burleigh had said about the rumours of the Hand. They originated in the taverns, stews and beargardens. This was not a movement of the nobility, no discontented political faction of ambitious noblemen who would follow the example of Elizabeth's grandsire, the young sprig of the Tudors who had risked the throw of the dice of fortune to seize the crown of England as Henry VII. Ambition was no doubt at the heart of it, ambition and greed, for the vision Nimue had sensed of the dark magic arising from the mention of the Hand had not been that of modesty or selflessness. But at the same time, there was something else about it that fitted in with what Will had said about a jealous God, something that would have prompted the involuntary movement of his fingers to touch the talisman at his throat. Something that would explain Burleigh's mention of the fearfulness with which his disreputable informants had revealed the vague rumours they had heard in the first place.

Nimue became more convinced as she sat beside her fire considering the matter, that somehow, the Hand was concerned with faith, with the bigotry and intolerance that sprang from spiritual arrogance, spiritual pride. Men went to war for their beliefs, and her father's stories of persecution in the reign of Bloody Mary came back with renewed significance to her mind. He had taken no joy in seeing the martyrs of any faith burn at Smithfield, but he had taught his daughter to be tolerant of the beliefs of others. There were many paths, he used to say, to Heaven. Indeed, he would pursue the matter further when speaking to those who could understand such concepts, and declare that there were also many heavens.

Now, Nimue realised uneasily that there might also be many hells, many Purgatories, and that if she had accepted when she agreed to undertake this task for Burleigh that she might be risking her immortal soul against the dark, how much more powerful than the threat of death might the threat of damnation and alienation from God prove to the ordinary people who were not versed in the intricacies of theology, of philosophy, of debate. Somewhere there was such a threat, she could sense it in her bones. And into her mind, unbidden, kept materialising the glimpse she had had of the man in the dark cloak, whose eyes had burned towards her with the secret blaze of wildness, of fanatisicm.

The Holy Devil, they called him, Will had said, and she could understand why. He was dangerous, but was the threat he embodied directed against the evils of wicked living, or of Popery (for he was obviously of some new faith, from the soberness of his garb and the Lady Ardua's preaching at the players)? Or did it go deeper than that? Was it he who posed a threat to the kingdom, and was it his personal greed and ambition that was at the root of the rumours of the Hand?

Nimue was roused from her musings as Huw entered her little parlour with his noiseless tread, his white robes glimmering in the twilight. He bowed before her. Though he could not speak, his tongue having been cut out as a child, yet he was able to project his thoughts into his young mistress's mind. Nimue had her own power, having been born the daughter of a wizard, but Huw had come from a burning land where the sun had scorched the skins of the people black, and his inherent mastery of magic and knowledge of arcane secrets was as deep.

As he bowed, his dark-skinned hands hidden within the sleeves of his robe, Nimue understood that she had a visitor awaiting her in the hall. She turned her head, wondering. It was almost dark, and the room was filled with shadows. Huw waited with impassive eyes, and Nimue rose.

'I will come.'

★ ★ ★

The girl who stood trailing her wet skirts of dark purple velvet in the dimness of the wainscoted hall, was shaking drops of rain from her hat. Its long feather had been reduced to a travesty of its once brave plume.

'Ruined!' she said ruefully, displaying the drooping cap. Then she smiled at Nimue. 'But it was worth it. I was determined to pay you a call.'

And as Nimue stood looking rather blankly at her, at a loss, she added quizzically:

'You do not remember me, I can see. Well, it is no wonder. I was a leggy colt of a girl when we last met, more like a callow youth, with straws in my hair.' She paused. Then, deliberately: 'But you will remember my mother. Jemima

Blackcross. Your father was once kind to her.'

A dim vision from the past came into Nimue's mind. Jemima Blackcross — a woman ailing and shrivelled, shivering feverishly within the folds of her plain woollen cloak, who had knocked at the door of Gereint Gwynne's house early one morning before the city was astir, as wraithlike as the mists that rose and swirled along the river until she spoke, and then her sharp northern turn of phrase had dispelled the illusion of magic. And, while she had sat with the burning eyes and hollow cough symptomatic of her ailment, earnestly talking with Nimue's father, the girl had watched over the child who had accompanied the visitor, and given it ale and cake. It had been, she recollected now, an awkward stick of a creature, neither boy nor girl, with dirty hair in a tangle round its face, wearing nondescript hose, much darned, and a tunic faded and shapeless from much washing, that had nevertheless still been too small. It had not spoken a word in spite of Nimue's encouragement and the friendly offer of a kitten, a warm bundle of black and white fur, purring throatily, to play with.

'Yes, I was that child. Rosalind Blackcross,' said the young woman, watching seemingly amused as Nimue groped for the memory. Then there was no laughter in her face. 'My mother was dying when she came to see the wizard Gwynne, and there was the shadow over us. He made it easier for her but she passed soon afterwards. And I — .' Then suddenly her face was shuttered, forbidding questions or sympathy. 'Well, I am here now. I survived her death. But I have not forgotten.'

As Nimue invited her to sit within the parlour and take refreshment, she was recalling what her father had said when the woman in the plain cloak had departed, taking her child with her. His face had been grave.

'A great loss, a wasted life,' had been

his comment when Nimue ventured that there seemed to be a sorrow, a cloud about the two of them. Nimue, as well as Gereint Gwynne, had seen intuitively that the woman was dying, and had assumed it was this which had prompted his remark but after a pause when his thoughts had been far from her, he had said:

'The saddest tragedy of all is when a soul consciously chooses the wrong path, Nimue. That woman might have been a shining light, a beacon, but her reckoning is about to be made. I am sorry for her because she knows it. Sometimes it is easier to remain in ignorance.'

Nimue had not understood his words then, and she did not really understand them now, though she sensed that there had been great trouble and difficulty for Rosalind Blackcross, left to fend for herself after her mother's death.

'Your father too is dead now, as well as my mother,' the girl said, recalling her to the rain-shadowed parlour where the wet branches were bowed weightily, blocking out the last of the evening light. 'I am sorry. He was a powerful man.'

There was a silence in the room, and then, as though a spell was being broken, light bloomed softly as Huw entered with his noiseless tread, a taper in his hand. He moved about lighting the candles, as though performing a solemn ritual, and Nimue felt an inexplicable easing of her heart as the shadows lifted. Outside the rain still whispered on the casement, and the far cries of the watermen were raucous and desolate as sea-birds calling. It was the mention of her father, she thought, that had provoked the melancholy mood. She made a conscious effort to shrug it off, and turned to see Rosalind Blackcross watching her across the rim of her wine cup.

Her mind had the awareness before it passed into her consciousness. Some-how, though her father had not told her so, she knew that Rosalind Blackcross's mother had possessed the powers. And there was something about the girl herself — . It was more than possible that the daughter had inherited them. For there were no coincidences. It was fate, chance, destiny, call it what you would, that had brought Rosalind to her.

In her inner vision once again, the figure of the man in the dark cloak materialised, and with rising expectation that thrilled through her, she realised that she had, perhaps, been given an unexpected ally.

Perhaps, even, Rosalind knew something of the Hand. Why had she come? Not just to offer her sympathy over Gereint Gwynne's death. There was some secret awareness in her face, a shutter over her eyes. Yet, mindful of Burleigh's warnings, unwilling to commit herself, Nimue stayed silent. How could she approach the subject? And then the words came to her without her own volition.

'I see you wear a talisman,' she

commented, indicating the shining chain about Rosalind's neck, on which there was an unpolished stone of the same dull purple as her skirt — an amethyst, perhaps. 'It is powerful.' In fact, the stone did draw her gaze. 'Does it guard against the plague? Or the Hand?'

'The Hand?' repeated Rosalind, after a moment.

'I have heard mention of some terrible fate that can at any time overtake the unwary. It is called the Hand of Glory, I believe,' Nimue said composedly, as though she exchanged the most frivolous of court gossip. 'It is the talk of the taverns I am told, but of course, since I am only recently in town from Wales, I have not heard all the details.'

Rosalind put down her cup. Her eyes glowed in the candlelight, reflecting the flames.

'Your father was a man of wisdom, a cunning man,' she said. 'Did he never hear mention of the Hand of

Glory? It is common belief that there is power in a dead man's hand. In fact,' she added, smiling, 'my talisman is not to guard against the Hand but to invoke it.'

Nimue felt her senses begin to thrum. The girl's presence in her parlour seemed suddenly charged with significance.

'You would invoke the hand of a dead man?' she queried.

'Oh, it is more than just a dead man's hand. It must be the hand of a man who has been hanged on a gibbet,' Rosalind told her. 'Such a hand holds powerful magic.'

'In what way? For is not death a release from the confines of the body and an entering into the spirit?' Nimue asked a little dubiously. There was something distasteful and ominous in the mention of dead men, men who had died on the gallows.

Rosalind's eyes challenged her.

'Oh, the original possessor of the hand is unaware,' she said deliberately.

'It must be cut from his corpse, pickled and dried in a manner that only the wise know. And then — .' Her voice was reverent. 'It holds the power of sleep.'

Nimue felt an unexpected frisson touch her skin. Her father had taught her that superstitions were born of ignorance and fear, and though the natural world often provided seemingly magical remedies for most ills, a hand severed from a corpse was surely an unlikely gift of nature. And yet, she thought fairly, did not the pious of all creeds venerate their relics, removed from the bodies of their holy men and women?

She looked closer at Rosalind, studying the girl's face. There were dark shadows smudging her eyes in spite of their brightness, and lines of tension in the set of her jaw and neck.

'You find it difficult to sleep?' she asked.

Was this, she wondered, why Rosalind had come to her, in the hope that she possessed her father's powers? But what was it that shadowed the young features, brought that dark glitter to her gaze? Nimue began to wonder about the cloud she had seen around the mother. Did the daughter carry it also? And what did it signify? To the mother it had meant death. What had the fates laid upon the daughter?

Rosalind averted her face and the candlelight glowed richly on her brown hair, burnishing it fiery red. Nimue was suddenly aware of how young she was. Her dress and manner were those of a poised young woman, but it had been only a few years ago that she had sat on Gereint Gwynne's hearth with her legs beneath the worn tunic as long and thin as a colt, shapeless and flat-chested and silent. Now her body had matured and there was knowledge in the curve of her mouth.

In the silence, as Rosalind did not answer, Nimue spoke again.

'Do you need my help?' she found herself asking dubiously, and the girl looked at her for a long moment.

'Oh no, I do not need your help.' Then her lips moved in a slight half-smile. 'But perhaps, mistress, you are in want of mine.'

3

The waters of the Thames were running softly somewhere in the rainy dark beyond her garden, and the scent of wild narcissus was pale and sweet, for Huw had placed a handful of the delicate flowers beside her pillow. Within the depths of the curtained bed, Nimue was dreaming.

She was standing alone on a high, rocky ledge, with rock beneath her feet, and outspread before her in the light of an early morning, mistwreathed and chill, was the sea. But it was not any sea she knew, not the wide estuary of the Dee that lay along the Welsh coast below Pendragon and Gilbert Stoneyathe's manor of Grannah where she had spent the last winter. Nor even the wider sea beyond the castle of Flint, beyond the towers of Rhuddlan and Conway.

This was an ocean, and the sky that raced above it was as wide and varied as the heavens themselves, with shifting light and a myriad shades of that light. Soft so that she could have wept from the beauty of it, neither blue nor yellow nor green was that light, not silver nor gold, but something of them all, and grey too like the feathers of a little bird. Here and there, strands of black light struck the surface of the sea and buried themselves in the waters that reflected the sky. The light filled her horizon, and on each side of her, great cliffs rose, the massive dark bulk of cliffs that lifted themselves sheer from the water, something to make the breath catch as they loomed upwards, silent, with shreds of mist making them unreal as cliffs that only existed within the mind, insubstantial. And somewhere, there was surely a ship — .

But even as she struggled to pierce the mists, to catch the glimpse of the sails, the dream had faded, and she had lost it. She opened her eyes to see the dark blue curtains of her bed in the wavering morning light, and felt the welcome warmth of her quilt, pulling it close about her with an involuntary shudder. The heaviness of it banished the buffeting of storm from the west, but there was a cry keening still, she seemed to hear it quivering on the air even as she lifted her head from her piled up, downy pillows in inexplicable alarm.

* * *

Storm. Ships lost at sea. A wild coast and the cliffs, the cliffs whose very name was a dirge of storm and tempest, isolation and death. And strange beauty that caught at the heart. The Cliffs of Moher. And beyond them, a far ocean.

She knew what had caused the dream, in all its disturbing vividness, of course. It had been the stories concerning that singular Irish woman she had met the previous evening, when she had been invited to attend a supper party at the house of Black Tom, the Earl of Ormond. The Queen's cousin through her mother's family, the Boleyns, the Earl was a man who had charmed Elizabeth with his silver-tongued Irish flattery, and remained very much in her favour. Nimue vaguely recollected hearing mention of him among reference to other Irish nobles and gentry when her father had commented, as he sometimes did, on the affairs of the day.

Since he counted himself an exile from his native country which, like Ireland, was ancient and Celtic, Gereint Gwynne had felt an affinity with any Irish rebels and declared, with a small smile, that it was beyond the capacity of any English head to understand, far less subdue, a race of Celts.

But 'the Black', as his own people called him, the Earl of Ormond, had the Irish ability to be more civilised, if he cared to do so, than the rest of civilisation put together, though

Nimue was not aware of this since she had never previously moved in such elevated ranks of society — or indeed, in any ranks of society at all. The flattering attentions of the young Lord Daventry, when he happened to call upon her father, had been her only acquaintance with lords or ladies. She was surprised — and not entirely happy — to discover that Rosalind Blackcross appeared to have the entree to court circles now, or some of them, at least, and at first she had been reluctant to accept the girl's casually proffered invitation to accompany her to supper at 'the Black's'. But Rosalind, moving her hand impatiently, assured her that she would be very welcome and also that she would find the gathering interesting.

'There are visitors from Ireland with whom you will have much in common,' she had said, watching Nimue. 'Two women in particular. One of them is unique, some sort of a Queen in her own kingdom, I believe, in the west.

Though she is old, as old as Her Majesty, she has for years captained her own galleys at sea, leading a crew of the most bloodthirsty savage sailors. A woman of distinction, would you not agree?'

Wondering a little why this woman should be of such importance to herself — or to Rosalind either — Nimue agreed that it was certainly unusual to find a woman, particularly a Queen of advancing years, captaining a ship and serving in her own navy in person.

'Though there have been warrior Queens before in these islands, and a tradition of fierce women in the old tales of our ancestry,' she added, for the sake of making conversation with her visitor. 'My father taught me of Boudicca, who defied the Roman invaders to these shores and led her troops in battle against them. And also Gwenllian of Wales, who in the absence of her husband was forced to lead her army to defend her estates.'

'But that is the very point I am

making,' said Rosalind, her eyes glittering in the candlelight. 'This woman, Granny Malley is her name, has had husbands, three of them I think, but she leads her adventurous life by her own choice, and she was bold enough to overthrow the Salic law that no female might take power as chief of her clan. She is powerful in her own right, not by courtesy of a man.'

'Like our own Queen,' Nimue commented, surprised and slightly amused by Rosalind's unexpectedly passionate display of feminism.

The other girl was silent for a moment, then she said in a different tone:

'Your father was a man of power. You are his daughter. Do you not consider yourself equal to ordinary men?'

'Ordinary men?'

Even as Nimue spoke, casually considering Rosalind's words, the remembrance came into her mind again of the figure she had seen in the tavern with Will, a dark cloak concealing its shape, the black hat and hair shadowing its features. Ordinary men, yes, she could hold her own with an ordinary man, but this man she could not even begin to fathom. The Holy Devil, the Counsellor? Who was he? And even more disturbing, what was he, in truth? Friend or foe? The dark magician behind the sinister images of the Hand, or — ?

She gave a little shrug. 'Ordinary men, perhaps, but — .'

'Then come with me,' Rosalind urged. 'I said you might require my assistance, did I not? You need introductions to the right people, you need — ,' and she laughed suddenly, carelessly: 'You need to be launched into society. I have my mother's powers, you know, and I have been accepted in the best circles for the sake of my gifts.' She faced Nimue with sudden intensity in her voice and eyes. 'Let me help you, for your father's sake, who let my mother find the peace to die — .' In the pause that followed, she added obliquely, so that Nimue wondered again what she knew, and whether she had an ally in her mission in the dark: 'And for your own sake. Do you not also have your place to find in the world, now that your father is dead?'

★ ★ ★

So she had been content to let the spirits of mysterious chance guide her, and with Math in attendance stood composedly, looking about her with interest in the unexpectedly tasteful chamber where the Earl of Ormond's guests were gathered. There was evidence here of the colour and richness she associated with Wales, and a harper was playing and singing in a language that was not Welsh, but had the same sense of magic to it. The wine she was drinking had the same flowery sweetness she had tasted in the quiet room in Pendragon tower where a great globe of the heavens glimmered softly and starry in the light of the candle flames.

She could feel the flood of remembrances sweep over her, and with them, the unbearable sensation of loss. She was weakened, vulnerable, and as she made an effort to lift her head, blinking back threatening tears fiercely, she caught the eye of a woman who was watching her. The woman's eyes were light and clear as a mirror, and in them Nimue saw her own self reflected, her own grief and confusion, and she had time to notice only the plain coif that framed the pale face severely before the woman looked away and the moment was gone. As she composed herself, Nimue thought there had been something meaningful and uplifting in the little exchange, and she was strangely comforted.

But there was a deeper expectation in the air, and Nimue was more than ever convinced that there was something for her here, some pointer, perhaps for her to follow. Rosalind had been recognised with evident pleasure, and Nimue, a little doubtful as to her reception, had been utterly disarmed by the pronunciation of some ancient welcome in the Irish tongue that had spread itself about her with the warmth of a beautiful cloak. She felt at ease immediately, but was aware of the punctilious and perfect courtesy that allowed her to retain her dignity and distance even while she was accepted as the most long awaited of guests. She found it very pleasant and easy, and as Rosalind had promised, the company assembled was unusually interesting.

Rosalind herself, wrapped in a decorative cape of blue that shimmered as though she had obtained the fabric from the twilit sky, moved secretively among the other guests with an unearthly look about her that seemed to Nimue, to encompass the whole gathering, guests and intimates of 'the Black'.

Perhaps it was that language they

spoke when they were not conversing formally in Latin or carefully accented English, she thought. She had managed to make herself familiar with the Welsh tongue when she had been in Wales, conscious that the silvery liquid sounds which seemed to have been created from the rushing of the waters of that land of streams and springs was the tongue her mother had spoken, which her father's voice had kept silent behind the English which was the currency of his adopted city of London. And too, it was the native language of her husband, the language of spells and magic, dreams and enchantment.

But these people from the far west, from the island which drifted beyond the sunset, spoke another magical tongue that throbbed like the sounds of birds, the golden notes that surely the sparrow-hawk or the doves of Venus herself would speak if they could. Nimue was aware of a sense of other-worldliness pervading the chamber, some sense that all was not what it seemed, and she found herself sharpening her critical faculties, her powers of reason. She knew Rosalind claimed to have inherited the abilities of her mother, but there was more in the undercurrents here tonight than the presence of a girl whose mother had been wise, who had inherited the ability to see with other eyes and work herbs for healing. There was something here that lay waiting, hidden, something she could feel but not identify.

And it was not 'the Black' himself who was responsible for it, the Earl of Ormond, whose Irishness had charmed Elizabeth and continued to do so. He was a consummate courtier who had learned to be both Irish and English, to be at ease and yet to keep his integrity among both his own people and the English lords who regarded him as a foreigner. He was very much his own man, but a man of this world.

Could her sense of expectation have been caused, she wondered, by the famed Irish Queen, the lady who commanded her own ships? She was almost a legend in her own country, apparently, her exploits the stuff of the harpers and ballad-mongers. Someone preciously attired in brown velvet, with a fastidious pomander on its chain at his breast and the carrying tones of an inveterate gossip, was heard to ask whether it was true that Granny Malley was truly more male than female, since she had lived all her life cheek-by-jowl with the most Godless of sailors. Was it true, he queried in tones of delicious horror, that she had actually given birth to her youngest child among her crew of ruffians on the deck of her vessel at sea?

Nimue, along with everyone else who had not already made the acquaintance of this formidable Irish lady, found her eyes drawn in fascination to the figure that entered when Grainne O'Malley was announced. It was obvious that she must have been the focus of gossip all her life, and been none the worse for it. And now, it seemed, she was about to crown her achievements so far as the English were concerned, by being received by the Queen of England to present her case regarding affairs in her own country.

Nimue wondered, with some curiosity, what Elizabeth would make of Grainne O'Malley. She was tall, taller than all the other women present (and taller than Elizabeth, which would not please Her Majesty). There was a vague resemblance to the Lady Ardua, in that she too was spare and active in her old age, but she was by no means as eccentric as the doubleted gentlewoman Nimue had encountered in the tavern with Will. The Irish Grainne was thinly drawn, the bones of her face arresting in their strange Celtic savagery beneath skin that was hard as old leather, tanned and roughened by sun, wind and sea. She seemed to bring the expanses of great oceans, the seas like those which Nimue had seen off the Welsh coast, into the suddenly over-civilised room with her; and the folds of her fine woollen cloak, muted in some lost, forgotten hue of ancient richness, fell from her bony shoulders over her plain gown as naturally as the leaves clung in summer to a branch. The white linen cap upon her head, rolled and folded in a manner Nimue had never encountered before, made a startlingly dramatic frame for the directness of her eyes, set in the deep sockets of that strangely unfeminine face.

Yet, the girl considered, as 'Granny Malley' was presented to some of the other guests, fascinating though this woman was, it was not from her that the undercurrents she sensed were flowing. Grainne O'Malley, like 'the Black', had her feet firmly set on the earth, for all that she probably possessed far more awareness of the heavens than the gentlefolk who gabbled their way through the fashionable rituals and services of the English church on Sundays.

Nimue was standing apart from the other guests, deep in her thoughts, when she became aware suddenly that the Irish woman was regarding her fixedly and speaking to a man at her side, who was listening with tilted head. He smiled, and bowed in Nimue's direction.

'Ah, lady,' he said in a voice that was deep and held the accents of Ireland. 'Is it from Ireland that you are? For sure, you are known to the daughter of Dubhdara Ui Mhaille, Grainne Ui Mhaille.'

Nimue, startled to see recognition in the woman's eyes, did not know what to answer.

'Tell my lady I am not of her country,' she said at length, wondering. 'I am of the Celtic descent, it is true but I was born in Wales, and I have no knowledge of Ireland.'

When the man translated this, Grainne O'Malley frowned as though puzzled, a network of fine wrinkles covering her face.

'She says, she has sure seen you at your daily tasks in Liscannor Bay and near the Cliffs of Moher,' the translator's voice went on, and Nimue would have answered that the Irish woman must have been mistaken, but a man in elaborate court dress burst into their small conversation, and with a brief apology, began to speak to Grainne and her escort about the political situation in Connaught. Nimue realised immediately that his foppish appearance was deceptive, and that his cool voice was more revealing of his true nature. She thought he might even have been one of Lord Burleigh's men playing a role in order to gain information without being suspected.

But what was Lord Burleigh's agent doing at this informal gathering? Unoffended, considering, Nimue turned speculatively away.

And following this, her dream.

Massive cliffs, lifting their bulk from the waves in ramparts that towered into the mist. Storm and ships lost, and the shifting light on a far sea. Liscannor Bay, the woman had said. Nimue knew nothing of it. The Cliff of Moher. Cliffs the Irish woman had also mentioned by name, which Nimue had never heard of and never seen. But in the vicinity of which she had somehow been known and recognised.

Later the following morning, she sat drinking her ale and eating a crumbly slice of game pasty. Her household tasks were done for the moment, and the kitchen given over to Mistress Grabbon, who had been appointed by Burleigh as her housekeeper. It was a novelty for Nimue to have servants of her own, and she was grateful to Burleigh for finding the beaming, pear-shaped goodwife who bustled so effectively and who found nothing strange in sharing her ministrations with an old man whose dark skin proclaimed his eastern ancestry, who in his enforced silence and the secrets of his body carried the marks of the slave-masters' knives, and whose eyes saw into the soul. Huw moved through the house soft-footed in his white robes, somehow aware of everything though he did not understand the English tongue, and he guarded the duties he considered his personal responsibilities for Pendragon's wife. Mistress Grabbon had even remarked that it did her heart good to have such an imposing person to consult, a house needed a man of authority in it.

The good lady's husband, Mister Grabbon was a mysteriously shadowy figure. Nimue did not know it (and neither did Mistress Grabbon), but he had for years served the cause of Elizabeth's intelligence system in various far-flung corners of Europe, so that his wife had only set eyes upon him three times in twenty-four years. However, she was possessed of a wonderfully stolid temperament, and had never yet bothered to query the business affairs (supposedly as a merchant of woollens, worsteds and sturdy cloths) which necessitated such prolonged absences from his hearth and home.

She behaved as though he was just out of sight, round the corner, and conducted long conversations with him regardless of the fact that they were, of necessity, one-sided, referring often to remarks 'he' had made and advice 'he' had mysteriously given to her during these interchanges, which were models of good sense and shrewdness. Mistress Grabbon greatly esteemed the counsel she obtained from her absent mentor, and often declared she did not know how she would manage without 'his' sound advice to guide her.

As she sat in the parlour, Nimue was aware of Mistress Grabbon's voice melodious in the kitchen, and she thought wryly that it was a pity she could not consult with the omnipotent Mister Grabbon concerning the events of the previous evening. And her dream. She had been known to a woman she had never seen, from a country she had never visited — and then she had been granted a vision of the same place in her sleep. What did it signify?

There was some deep import here, but she reminded herself that she must not allow her attention to be diverted from her mission concerning the Hand. Yet, were they unconnected? It was Rosalind who had invited her to 'the Black's' to meet Grainne O'Malley — . Rosalind who she was certain had some ulterior motive, who might yet prove to be her ally, to help her confront the dark magic. And perhaps too, to confront the dark man, if she had to. The man in the black cloak and hat who sat so still in the corner of the tavern. The man whose very presence was like the forming of a thunder-head in the summer sky, stirring the air with dangerous force.

As she reflected, she recalled suddenly the second woman Rosalind had wanted her to meet and had briefly presented her to. It had been the woman with the coifed face and reflective eyes who had been looking at her when she thought of the past, and the room with the starry globe in Pendragon tower. Another Irishwoman, but very different to Grainne O'Malley. A sister of the Church, Nimue had assumed, since she wore the severe robe and coif of some Order, and her face was almost stern, the light eyes holding depths that were not immediately apparent. Nimue sensed great power, and had not quite grasped the name Rosalind pronounced, she had been absorbed momentarily in an awareness of the woman's still forcefulness. Maire Maeve of — where had it been? Somewhere else which would mean nothing to her. The woman had regarded her coolly, unsmiling, but that was all, and Nimue had been addressed by someone else and turned away. When she was able to turn back, Rosalind and Maire Maeve had moved on.

But perhaps Rosalind, aware of some sort of need for spiritual power, had wanted Nimue to meet someone else who had the necessary strength to confront the dark. Perhaps she was not as alone as she had thought. Yet the girl was still troubled by the sense of — something — which she felt hovering just beyond her awareness. She could trust no-one. Except the man who had instructed her on the task she must carry out — .

★ ★ ★

It had been arranged that if Nimue had any occasion to give information to Lord Burleigh or make any form of contact with him, she would first call upon an apothecary in the Strand, where she would enquire whether she might purchase a gram of the substance known as Dragon's Head.

'And then?' Nimue had queried, when the arrangements were made. Burleigh had smiled thinly.

'You will know in due course, when you follow this procedure, Mistress Pendragon.'

And so, with Math watchful at her shoulder, here she was in the afternoon tramping through the mud of the narrow city streets, her cloak pulled high about her face against the rain. London — and indeed, the whole country — had seen no sun for months, it was a year when the hand of God seemed to lay even heavier upon the people than in the previous years of plague, and there was a sense of futility everywhere, as though the sun would never shine again. Men talked of the ruin of crops, of the failure of harvest, and everywhere there were faces to be seen which were thin and gaunt. Nimue thought also of the unseen but threatening presence of the Hand — that which caused men to cross themselves in fear, voices to sink to whispers. And even bold, devil-have-'em individuals like Will Shakespeare to go still and silent in constraint. It was something equally as evil as any creeping pestilence, and it was upon her slender shoulders, her burden to carry for those who could not. She could not afford to fail.

They found the place in the wider

thoroughfare of the Strand, and Nimue stepped into the small dark room where the apothecary might be found. And boldly requested the ancient who wheezingly enquired as to her business, to furnish her, if he would be so kind, with a gram of Dragon's Head. She did not quite know what she expected, but without looking up from the musty pages where he was consulting the script through spectacles of glass that slid low on his bony nose, the ancient replied that he would have the substance ready in the morning at the hour of eleven, and bade her return for it then. Nimue inclined her head gravely (having, after all, no choice in the matter), and said she would do so. Then she and Math splashed through the mud to refresh themselves at an eating-house, one of the many 'ordinaries' where the citizens of the city might enjoy cheer and company.

Nimue forgot the discomfort of her soaked cloak and muddied gown, as well as her chilled wet feet, in the warm, steamy atmosphere, and she was glad to taste hot food. And afterwards, instead of commencing the journey home, she decided on the impulse — since they were near the place — to pay another call.

When she had fled in such haste from North Wales on the night of the fire, she had been newly and secretly married. The husband to whom she had never yet gone as a bride, renowned as a man of deep and secret power as his father had been before him, had been the scapegoat for the desperation and anger of men who had been robbed of their homes, their livelihoods, even their families, by grasping landowners. It had been a mob of dispossessed Welsh who had attacked Pendragon tower and set it alight in their impotent fury over social injustice. They had been unable to strike at the true source of their wrongs.

But it was men like Gilbert Stoneyathe, eaten up by his greed for land, who were the real authors of the violence — and who might even act violently themselves. Nimue had been thinking over the events that had led up to that terrible night, and now that she had had time to reflect, she realised more than ever that she badly needed advice. Her father's words, always with her, would guide her in the ways of the spirit, but in the ways of the world she was an inexperienced child.

Her father had occasionally mentioned the name of Ruffard Rowland, whom he had consulted on any matters of law, and Nimue knew his house was near the Strand. She took a chance and had Math knock for admittance. Mister Rowland was, she was informed, at home and before she had considered exactly what to say to him, she was shown into a small chamber with a window that looked out onto a tiny court where doves sat like silver images as the rain ran down their white feathers.

It was a pleasant sight and Nimue relaxed somewhat as she was courteously served with refreshment and the man with the watchful eyes waited for her to state her business.

'I need your counsel, sir,' she said at last, though she hardly knew where to begin. 'You advised my father I know, and he valued your advice. After his death I — went to Wales, where I was married. My — my husband had estates in Flintshire.'

'Had?' The word was quietly spoken.

'He is dead,' Nimue said evenly, without looking at him. 'Events were — somewhat confused and frightening. My husband's house was burned by protesters against the enclosure of common lands, and he — he perished in the fire. I had cause to return to London immediately, the same night, and I came away leaving all in the care of my husband's old friend.'

After a pause: 'There is more, I think,' suggested Mister Rowland shrewdly, and Nimue nodded.

'Indeed, there is. I believe that a man

committed murder. I have no proof, no evidence — .' Her voice wavered uncertainly. Her father had warned her often:

'There are times when your vision will burden you, child. This world does not turn by the truth as you and I see it.'

And now Mister Rowland's eyes sharpened and narrowed before they went carefully blank.

'That is a very serious allegation, Mistress Pendragon.'

'I know,' Nimue said steadily, adding: 'Even more serious because the man concerned is not a common criminal. He holds a high social position, and is responsible to many who look to him to set an example.'

There was another pause, then Mister Rowland repeated slowly: 'You have no proof, you say.'

'No.' Nimue said no more. She felt it would be imprudent to reveal details at this stage, of the existence of gold on the Pendragon land, the rock seamed with fire which proved it and the fact that she had heard Gilbert speak with Ralph Tollaster, the bailiff whose body lay now, no doubt, in some hasty grave in the churchyard at Grannah. Gilbert had taken the rock, she knew that, but she knew also that he would deny its very existence. There was nothing, nothing save her own account of the rock that Pendragon had shown to her, the fact that she had heard Tollaster tell Gilbert of it and that she had seen them ride out together and Gilbert, white-hot with some suppressed emotion, return alone. And that, just before the news came of Tollaster's murder, she had seen Gilbert examining the rock in his chamber — and the look in his eyes when they had ridden in with the body.

Nothing, she saw now, could ever be proved. Nor could she reveal how Gilbert and Mary and Dorabella Mowas, who was soon to become Gilbert's wife, had been ready to accuse her of the murder, of witchcraft, out of their complicity of guilt, spite and fear.

She spread her hands helplessly, looking up at the notary with troubled eyes.

'I apologize, sir. Heresay and suspicion, I will say no more about the matter.'

'It would be best, perhaps, to confine yourself to facts, the facts of estate business,' he agreed after a moment. 'If you would care to let me have the details, I can communicate with the authorities in Flintshire and arrange your affairs more properly in your absence from the Principality.'

'Yes,' Nimue said, 'yes, I will review the matter and return to you, sir.'

'I will await your instructions, Mistress Pendragon,' he said gravely, and moved to escort her from the chamber. As she was leaving, he said quietly:

'Facts are facts, proof is proof, but do not forget, Mistress Pendragon, that justice in this realm is for all.'

His eyes were bright, and, somewhat

reassured by this covert message that he was perhaps more sympathetic towards what she had said than he had openly allowed, she went out with Math into the rain again.

4

'It is the hour of eleven, sir. I have come for my gram of Dragons Head.'

The old apothecary, his thin limbs in their tattered worsted folded, spiderwise, over his parchments, spectacles etched across his bony nose, did not look up, but a measured voice spoke from a dark recess beyond the arras.

'I have it safely for you, Mistress Pendragon. Will you enter?'

The man who stood there was stocky, his doublet dark and plain. Nimue had wondered since the previous day on what sort of substance might be produced when she returned to the apothecary's shop, and she did not hesitate. Inclining her head and with a word to Math, she passed through the doorway where the arras curtain hung, into an inner chamber. It was windowless, but a taper revealed warmth and even luxury, a table, wine in a silver jug, and two silver cups. There was a stool beside the hearth, where a small fire crackled cheerfully, and Nimue eyed it with some relief. Even the Strand had been a quagmire, the weather that morning more like November than March, and she was sodden with rain, raw with chills that had crept even into her youthful bones.

She looked about her for the substance she was to receive, and the man's lips moved slightly, but it was a mere courtesy, lacking in warmth. Something about the disinterested thinness of his expression reminded her of Lord Burleigh.

'The apothecary has prepared a packet for you, which will validate your visit here,' he stated, and placed a small twist of parchment on the table. She saw it was sealed with red wax. 'But we assumed your real purpose was to have speech with us privately. Be seated, mistress, and take your ease. Permit me.'

He took her cloak and hung it on a peg, then sat down himself, pouring wine into a cup for her with economy of movement. Then as she did not reply, he looked up rather impatiently.

'I am Robert Cecil,' he told her. 'Lord Burleigh is my father. I am in his confidence and here on his behalf. You may speak freely to me.'

But Nimue was still silent, sipping the excellent wine he proffered while she considered the situation. She could see now that though his clothes were plain, they were extremely rich, the dark materials very fine. He was in middle age, but he had, she thought, probably never really been young. He had been born an old man, with no time for a child's playing, his finger from his earliest years itching to meddle importantly in the pies of his father's official business. Robert Cecil. She had heard something of him. He was destined for greatness it appeared, both for the sake of his father's service to

Elizabeth and to the state, and on his own merit.

Yet she was reluctant to confide in him. She could see that unlike Lord Burleigh, who would have been prepared to accept whatever she might have felt it necessary to mention as of relevance, his son would only be made impatient by the mention of dreams or visions.

But she needed information and perhaps advice. Nimue decided, after a moment, to begin with indisputable facts.

'I have heard gossip concerning the Hand, sir, the Hand of Glory, which I was instructed to seek out,' she said. 'It is believed by the credulous that a dead man's hand, from one who has died on the gibbet, when pickled and secretly attended, will invoke sleep.'

Robert Cecil folded his arms. There was a lofty expression on his face that was almost — though not quite — a sneer.

'Indeed, mistress? There is more to

it than that,' he told her repressively. 'It is also the custom, among the criminal fraternity, to place candles at the finger-ends, or pitch them and then fire the dead man's hand so that it burns with five flames. It is carried as a torch, and used to light the way for those who would rob the houses of honest citizens. Or so,' he added in a dismissive manner, 'they say.'

There was silence. Then he gave a slight shrug, tolerant.

'That is your Hand of Glory, Mistress Pendragon. The burning fingers of a man who has died on the gibbet do indeed invoke sleep. They have the power to put all the members of a household into the deepest slumber, leaving thieves able to roam freely and help themselves to all the valuables they can find. Or so,' he added again with the same condescension, 'they say.'

Nimue looked into his set face. He was impassive, revealing no emotion.

'We have known of this, of course,' he told her, shrugging again. 'It is common knowledge.'

'Lord Burleigh knew, and he did not tell me?' Nimue asked, too intrigued to be offended at such deviousness. 'But if he knew the secret and meaning of the Hand of Glory, if it is known sir, then what purpose — ?'

'Because, Mistress Pendragon,' Robert Cecil interrupted with an exaggerated patience, as though he spoke to a child, 'it is obvious that this superstition, this Hand of Glory cannot be the Hand we seek if it is known to all, if it is parleyed among the frequenters of — forgive me, madam — .' His nostrils were pinched suddenly, overly fastidious.' — of stews and gambling dens. Places where the 'coney-catchers', as they fancy to call themselves, though common tricksters and criminals are the more accurate terms, gather to plot their undertakings against the honest man — if these are full of the Hand of Glory, then where is the threat, the portentousness that would make it whispered of in fear, and with fingers crossed against the evil eye? No, it is obvious — ,' and he smote a balled fist into the palm of his other hand, lightly, but with controlled violence that startled Nimue. 'The true Hand of Glory that hides its face behind this ancient custom is something more, something deeper, more sinister. The upright might fear a Dead Man's Hand, but not the lower orders. Mark me, Mistress Pendragon, this is the way of it.'

Nimue, considering, saw that he was right. She recalled how Will's fingers had moved as though he would touch the charm that hung at his throat, how his clear gaze had clouded. He too must have heard rumours beyond the superstitious practices of thieves and vagabonds. But what rumours?

She frowned as she considered further. Will, she was sure, would have told her anything he knew, anything that could have been explained, reported. His uneasiness had sprung — as her own conviction of dark magic had sprung — from intuition rather than factual evidence. People could feel it, if there was some threat in the air. They themselves gave it form, their fears brought it to a physical existence. It was this lack of certainty, this subtle, inexpressible sensation of menace that would account for the reactions that seemed to be occasioned by any mention or rumour of the Hand.

Something symbolic, perhaps, she pondered, forgetting Robert Cecil momentarily. Something that gave expression to a concept that could not otherwise be described. Nimue began to feel a certainty of it. She was sure, on consideration, that Will — and probably most of the men Robert Cecil had described, the lower sort of rogues whose haunts were the taverns and dens of excess — had no real idea of what the true threat might be. It hung, shapeless like a cloud, intangible. Something, though, that touched their sense of soul, of identity. Something of such moment that it could realistically be accredited for the signs and portents that appeared to foretell doom, the plague, the cold touch of the left hand of God.

* * *

Apart from the sort of talk that Robert Cecil, she was sure, would have greeted with painfully polite distaste — lifted brows, weary patience with a hysterical female's unfortunate over-emotionalism — there was one question that Nimue felt she might approach without apology. She mentioned the recent supper party she had attended at 'the Black's', and said that she had noticed a man who had seemed very interested in events in Ireland, to the point of rudeness. He had broken into her conversation with the Irish Queen Madame O'Malley, who was also present, and although he had been foppishly dressed, his manner and voice had belied his soft appearance.

She suspected, she told Robert Cecil calmly, that this man had also been working for Lord Burleigh as a government spy, and asked point-blank if this was so. She was wondering, she further explained, what his business might have been at the supper party. She herself had been invited by an acquaintance, someone who remembered her father with gratitude, and her presence had been entirely by chance.

She made no mention of the fact that she had been aware of deep undercurrents beneath the surface of the apparently innocent gathering, nor that it had provoked disturbing half-images she could not, for the moment identify. She did not feel Robert Cecil would be interested in her increasing conviction that Rosalind Blackcross had had some other motive than a desire to help her find a place in society, when she had pressed her invitation to attend and to meet Grainne O'Malley and the other guests. And as for the rest — the fact that the Irishwoman had so strangely noticed her, and that she had had a dream laden with mystery and significance — . All of these might or might not have a connection with the Hand and the dark power Nimue could not penetrate, that obscured her inner vision, but she knew she would lose her listener's attention altogether if she insisted on detailing them now.

As she sipped gratefully at her cup of wine, her chilled limbs began to relax and warmth to seep through her. It was a great pity that Lord Burleigh's son had decided he had no intention of taking either her or whatever she might say seriously, and she thought with regret that if she had known about his attitude in advance, and that this was how her reports would be received, she would have insisted on seeing Lord Burleigh himself. However, she had made the journey twice now through the rain and weather, and she did not intend to let this scornfully superior being intimidate her. He was undoubtedly his father's son — but was she not also her father's daughter?

At the mention of the man she had seen at 'the Black's', she saw, as she had expected, that Robert Cecil's mouth curved into a slight, condescending smile. It was obvious that he did not like women, nor feel at ease in their company. It was also abundantly clear to Nimue by now that he had no faith that she might challenge — far less overcome — the threat of the Hand, for he did not recognise her powers. Unlike his father who, though a realist, was wise enough to be aware that there were things beyond the capacity of human understanding, Robert Cecil was limited by fear of failure in the eyes of the world, and stubbornly refused to recognise abstracts he could not explain.

Watching him as he paused, measuring his words before speaking, Nimue felt, unexpectedly, a stab of pity. This man would always walk in the shadow of his father. He would never achieve the eminence of his parent, nor William Cecil's greatness as a statesman. When he spoke at last, his words increased her conviction.

'A spy! Woman-like, you use exaggerated terms, Mistress Pendragon,' he drawled, and Nimue sighed inwardly. She had not come all this way to play games designed to give Mister Robert Cecil comforting reassurances of his superiority, but because she was young, because she was slim and pretty even in her plain gown and cloak of mourning, he was dismissing her — as Gilbert had been inclined to do — as of little account, in spite of the fact that his father had (however reluctantly) been prepared to trust her good sense.

Nimue checked the words that came to her lips, which would only antagonise him further. An oft-quoted maxim of her father's came to her aid. 'It is always easy to recognise those with true power, Nimue, for they are the ones who never make any show of it'. So deliberately, aware of the amusement it would have caused both her father and her husband, she altered her manner, agreeing humbly:

'Indeed, sir, I would be grateful for your guidance. I am unfamiliar with such weighty business as I have been asked to undertake by your father Lord Burleigh — and deeply honoured by the confidence of Her Majesty. I ask myself in the privacy of my chamber, sir, whether I can even attempt to fulfil this task I have been set. Sometimes, sir, I have such doubts as to my abilities that I feel your father's confidence and Her Majesty's might have been misplaced, though I would never for a moment dream of doubting their judgement, and I tell myself that in their wisdom, they considered me worthy. I can only pledge to do my best, in the earnest hope that — .'

'Yes, yes, I can understand that,' Robert Cecil interrupted with a sharp frown. Women's vapours embarrassed him. 'But I am sure you will do admirably, Mistress Pendragon. Why, a less careful person might never have noticed the presence of our — agent — at the supper party you attended. It does you credit, madam, be assured.'

'He was an agent of the crown then?' Nimue enquired respectfully. 'I thought there must be some intent behind the gentleman's presence, but naturally, knowing nothing of the Irish situation — .'

'That is only to be expected, Mistress Pendragon,' Robert Cecil told her, becoming a little more expansive. 'Indeed, how could you know?'

'And Madame O'Malley, the Irish Queen — ,' Nimue began, with an air of impressionable earnestness, 'who is in England to present her case to Her Majesty, I understand, and who sails in her own ships? Naturally I took it for granted that all would seek to discourse with her for her own sake, not just to gain information — .'

She hesitated, a sudden intuition prompting her next remark. In her dream, there had been a ship somewhere, lost in the mist. And a wild western coast. Without knowing exactly what she was going to say, she began to speak in a different tone, low, her eyes wide and inward-looking. She was once again unaware of the presence of Robert Cecil:

'How well I remember the year of the Spanish fleet, when I was priviledged to assist my father at the behest of our Queen, to protect England against invasion. Storm came to scatter their might and I heard afterwards that the galleons were driven far off their courses, to meet terrible fate. Some were wrecked off the shores of Scotland, and some off Ireland — . Of course, if I had a man's greater ability, I might understand more, but I cannot for the life of me see what connection there could be between Spanish galleons and the presence of Madame O'Malley at court.'

In the silence that followed her words, the sound of the street criers and the bustling city, though muted by the rain, echoed faintly in the chamber, as though it came from a long distance away. Robert Cecil was staring at Nimue with suspicion in his face.

'Who told you of this, Mistress Pendragon?' he demanded coldly.

She turned a candid gaze on him, her green-gold eyes clear and without guile, like the eyes of a child.

'Your pardon, Mister Cecil, I was not concentrating but speaking my thoughts aloud.'

'The Spanish connection. You mentioned the Spanish fleet — Spanish galleons — but it is of course known to all that Ireland could be the back door to any planned invasion of England,' he muttered uneasily, as though he tried to convince himself. 'It is one of Her Majesty's most constant fears, and many times has been tried — . Wales of course, but if not Wales, Ireland.'

The random thought came into Nimue's head that it was no wonder Elizabeth was overly conscious of the threat from invasion. Such an invasion by her grandsire, who had marched from his landing in Pembroke to challenge Richard Plantagenet at Bosworth Field, had established the whole Tudor dynasty — and Elizabeth herself — upon the English throne. But she said nothing, for the turn the conversation had taken was far too interesting. She had indeed been prompted by an inner voice when she had mentioned the Spanish fleet, for it had not occurred to her consciously to connect Grainne O'Malley and her Irish seafaring activities with Spain.

'After the attempted invasion by Spain was repulsed, there were no less than twenty-six galleons wrecked off the coasts of Ireland,' Robert Cecil was saying now, his eyes withdrawn and distant. There was a cloud of worry in them, and a fine, sharp line between his brows. 'We heard reports of huge armies of Spanish soldiers, stranded and massing against us, in league with the Irish malcontents, not to mention tales of the fabled treasures carried by those same galleons — . The result, in spite of our constant alertness, and patrolling of the Irish coastline, has been predictable. Trouble, Mistress Pendragon, trouble.'

Nimue nodded gravely, relieved that his mood had changed. Reassured of her proper deference to his position, and perhaps, she thought, recollecting the contribution she had helped her father make towards the averting of the Spanish threat, he had begun to accept her as a colleague, however inept. For a moment, at any rate, while he was lost in his thoughts. She remained discreetly silent, lest she lose the advantage she had won.

For his part, Robert Cecil was relaxing. A sensible child after all, he thought; and though he considered that the Queen (who was also a female, and therefore prone to lapses of judgement in his opinion, though he would of course have died rather than allow his opinions to be made public) might have been swayed by superstitious prejudice when she appointed this daughter of a so-called wizard to her service, the girl also had the complete confidence of his father. The younger Cecil was not always in agreement with Lord Burleigh, but even he could not deny the older statesman's genius for statecraft.

And now the young woman in question was looking at him straightly, with none of the usual female primpings and preenings. He reminded himself suddenly that she wore the garb of a widow, and noted with reluctant approval that she conducted herself with great dignity, for all her grace of youth.

And then, surprising himself as well as Nimue, he smiled. It was something Robert Cecil did not often do, unless the smile was of condescension.

'Mistress Pendragon, your intuitive powers, like your esteemed father's, have seen to the truth of the matter. There is always trouble in Ireland, and the lady Grainne O'Malley, being Irish and being also of remarkable character and influence in her own passionate country, is a person of great interest to us — that is to say, the state is interested in her opinions and intents, and the means by which she — or indeed others of her country — might put their intentions into practise.'

Gratifyingly, she received this information with due gravity, and considered it carefully before she enquired:

'Is it then suspected that she — or any other power in Ireland — is involved in further Spanish invasions, sir?'

He tapped with his fingers on the surface of the table, frowning now into some unseen distance.

'Who can say, who can say, Mistress Pendragon?' Then suddenly, unexpectedly, he turned his gaze squarely upon her.

'My father esteems you and your powers highly. Can you indeed look into the crystal as others of your kind, and give me answers?'

Nimue was taken aback, but realised after a moment that in Robert Cecil, the bare facts would always war with a frustration to know more, and result in fluctuations of mood such as this. At the present, the man before her was open to anything she might say — but later, he would squirm that he had even considered listening to her.

'My father was an astrologer sir,' she said mildly, turning to the fire as though the warming of her hands was of more import to her than his question. 'He taught me to consult the stars, it is true, and the charts will give answers, though they require time and thought and working by one more skilled than I. Her Majesty also bade me look with the Sight concerning the Hand, yes, but I told her, as Doctor Dee and the rest have told her, that I could see nothing. The vision is obscured, there is only darkness. It may happen by fateful chance or — and this I think is the cause — it may be done with deliberate intent, by some dark source of power which is unwilling for any to witness its activities.'

Robert Cecil, absorbed in his thoughts, nodded a frowning acknowledgement of her words. He was aware of what Elizabeth's other advisers had said.

'I am sure that the threat is not as obvious as an invasion,' Nimue told him, after a moment. 'Would men cross themselves at the thought of Spanish ambition, or murmur, as you have remarked yourself, about omens and portents and the hand of God?'

Robert Cecil looked up, seeming surprised by her logic.

'Quite so, quite so,' he muttered.

'You will ask me what then it may be,' Nimue went on slowly. 'I wish I could tell you sir, but all I know as yet is that it concerns men's souls, perhaps, more than their bodies. And that — .' She paused, struck by intuitive certainty, then added: 'You are right to look to Ireland.'

'Ah,' said Robert Cecil, drawing a sharp, triumphant breath.

Nimue repeated as though to herself:

'The Cliffs of Moher — Liscannor Bay — . Sir, have you knowledge of them? I think Madame O'Malley knows them, and she mentioned them to me.'

'In what connection?' Cecil demanded with immediate suspicion, but Nimue moved her hand in a slight, negative gesture.

'It was nothing definite, sir. She thought she knew me — but she had mistook me for another, one who she said she had seen near the Cliffs of Moher — .'

He stared. His eyes were hard with calculation.

'Mistook you, Mistress Pendragon? You mean, she thought you were someone else? Some Irishwoman?'

'Yes, sir,' Nimue said simply.

Robert Cecil's heavy features had taken on colour. There was a new sense of alertness in him, like a hound that has sniffed the scent.

'A simple mistake for a stranger to make, madam. The lady was deceived.'

Nimue gave him back look for look, composedly.

'Do you believe so, sir?' she asked. 'I have never been in Ireland.'

He turned away at that, a shutter closing down on his face, leaving it expressionless.

'The Cliffs of Moher, you said? And Liscannor Bay?' He paused, considering. 'Did she mention anything further? Say, for instance, who it was that she had — um — mistook you for?'

'No sir, your other agent interrupted us at that moment,' said Nimue, and he looked irritated, as though she had bested him. He stirred officiously, seeming to distance himself from her, an indication she thought wrily that the confidences were obviously over. She sat waiting, feeling it would do no good to add anything further — and indeed, what could she really tell him? That she had had a dream?

'I do not think Madame O'Malley spoke with any ulterior meaning, sir,' she found herself saying thoughtfully. 'She was genuinely confused. It is not her you must watch, though she has the guile of her craft and the heart of a warrior.'

Robert Cecil stared at her for a long moment, then spoke formally.

'Come back in ten days, Mistress Pendragon, at the same hour, and we will discourse further.'

'Yes, sir,' said Nimue with proper deference, rising from her stool.

'You have done very well,' he added repressively, and she inclined her head.

'Thank you.'

★ ★ ★

No sooner had she and Math emerged into the mud and bustle of the Strand, and she was hesitating, considering whether to pay another call on Ruffard Rowland, than a piercing voice hailed her. Turning, she saw the long, lanky figure of the Lady Ardua, rain streaming down her brindled thatch of hair and rusty jerkin, bearing down upon her.

'Mistress Pendragon! I see,' Lady Ardua observed approvingly, 'that I have indeed been mistaken in you. It is to your credit, child, that you have made the journey through the weather to warm yourself at the fire of good counsel. I am abject, mistress.'

Before Nimue could express her bewilderment, her arm was seized, and though Math was at her shoulder in a moment, his hazel eyes alight, Lady Ardua merely raised her brows at him, said deliberately: 'Make way fellow, *if* you please,' and twitched Nimue through the soaking traffic and into the shelter of an overhanging house. As though he had been waiting for her, a dark figure turned and Nimue's knees went suddenly weak as she looked directly into the eyes of the Counsellor, the Holy Devil.

She supposed afterwards, when she was more able to consider the matter clearly, that she had deliberately been turning her mind away from the man because she had known, deep within her, how she would react when eventually — inevitably, she might have said — they met face to face. She had felt his power even at a distance, in the tavern with Will's solid presence beside her. Now it seemed to hit her like a blow, so that she all but reeled.

'Sir,' she began weakly, then turning to the Lady Ardua, who was still holding her arm, 'My lady — .'

But before Ardua could make any further comment — which Nimue had no doubt she would have done if she had not been so forestalled — the man spoke. Quietly, without raising his voice, and with an accent Nimue could not identify. She thought afterwards it might have been Dutch, or German, for she was vaguely familiar with such tongues, her father sometimes having had occasion to meet with merchants of the Hanseatic League, who had their own little colony in the city.

'The soul is weary and walks apart in

a dark place. You are stronger than you think, my daughter, yet weaker than others believe. I rejoice that you have seen fit to come to me — for by the power invested in me, I will console you and comfort you, I will bring you out of the dark into the light, and wipe away your tears.'

'Amen,' said Lady Ardua loudly.

After a stunned moment, Nimue made an effort to recover herself, and pulled her arm deliberately from the woman's grasp. Her mouth was dry and her heart racing, but she told herself firmly that she was *not* afraid. It was broad daylight in a public place, and Math was there, his hand stilled on his dagger, eyes intent as he looked at the two, the cloaked man and the mad old woman, waiting only to see whether she would give him the word. She smiled at him, trying to appear reassuring.

'It is quite all right, Math. Lady Ardua is in error.'

And how many more people were

going to mistake her, she wondered, with sudden annoyance that had the effect of releasing her from the paralysis that had held her in its grip. She straightened the sleeve which had been disarranged by Lady Ardua's predatory hand, carefully avoiding the shadowed eyes beneath the sweep of the man's wide hat.

'Pardon me, my lady,' she said as briskly as she could to Ardua. 'I am here on private business. I have not come for counselling.'

'Yet,' insinuated the man's voice, though Nimue was still very guardedly not looking in his direction, 'do you not need a light to guide you, woman, a warmth to brighten the coldness and emptiness that cannot be filled? I can see that it is so — ah, the wound bleeds yet, and the tears choke you though you defy them valiantly.' His tone was almost a whisper, and in spite of herself Nimue strained to catch it. 'Be counselled, accept the balm I will give you. Open your heart to me, that

I may make you whole again.'

Catching her breath, Nimue turned at last summoning all her resources and faced him squarely. The Counsellor. The Holy Devil. She knew now — oh yes, she knew why they called him a devil, those who feared him. He was a man not a demon, yet he was possessed of such strange power that could reach out with a few words, as though he had extended his hand. His low voice had touched her, closely and intimately, against her every instinct, making mock of all her defences.

Yet he himself remained invisible, featureless behind the black curling beard and long black hair, masked by his wide hat and the high collar of his cloak. Of course, she told herself, all men were obliged to protect themselves against this unseasonable weather, the never-ending rain, but it was impossible with this man to see beyond the cloak, to guess anything about him in spite of his imposing presence and his height. He might be young or old. His hands, she saw too, were gloved, and his voice and eyes were impressions only.

Nimue found herself wondering with quick, shameful curiosity that she instantly and firmly repressed, what he would look like when he removed the cloak and hat and gloves, whether he was young, lithe and supple, or had a wrinkled neck, gnarled rough knuckles and stiffness in his joints. She wondered also, briefly but grimly, whether the fascination that had gripped her was yet another result to the dark magic that blocked knowledge of the activities of the Hand — or whether this man simply enjoyed the exercise of his power over women. She had heard of other supposed men of the cloth whose tastes were regrettably unspiritual — running to female curves and the secret indulgences of the flesh.

A sudden passionate contemptuousness came to her aid, curling her lip with scorn.

'If you know ought of me, sir, you will be aware that I was recently widowed,' she said steadily, though there was fire in her cheeks and her eyes blazed golden-green. 'Naturally I am mourning my husband. But though I thank you, I cannot accept your offer to console me in my grief. I prefer to leave that to God.'

And cuttingly — though she regretted afterwards that she had allowed him to provoke any reaction at all, far less one that was so extreme — she turned on her heel and stepped deliberately into the traffic, splashing her skirts and provoking a curse from a horseman who had to tug his mount's head sharply away and swerve to avoid running her down. She stalked away stiffly without looking back, but was uncomfortably aware of the eyes that followed her into the thoroughfare, the wet crowds, the street sellers, the noise and the eternal mud. Math followed her like a shadow, silent, a pace behind.

The colours of the street whirled in glittering arcs before Nimue's eyes, and angrily she lifted a hand to dash away tears. She wanted to run from them all, to shut herself in her chamber and be alone with the suddenly revived ghosts of her past. She had thought she had confronted her grief, overcome it, but this man had revealed to her how weak were her defences, how fragile was her peace. He had spoken only a few words, but with them he had churned up her emotions so that the pain swelled almost unbearably.

She was burning, and she turned her face into the drizzle, doggedly and tried to shut her mind to the dark space of her husband's loss, the emptiness, as she plodded unseeing down the Strand towards the river.

★ ★ ★

As always, it was her father's image and the memory of his wise counsel that revived and steadied her. Dismissing Math, she went to her chamber when they returned home in the late afternoon, and retrieved from the press the worn leathern satchel which was all she had brought with her from North Wales on the night of the fire. It had been her father's, and the contents Nimue had as yet not touched, except for the great crystal, wrapped in its silken cloth, to which she had turned often for strength and inspiration particularly in the months after her father's death before she had wedded Pendragon, when she had felt herself lost and vulnerable in a strange land.

Now, she lifted the crystal carefully from the satchel and placed it gently on the polished boards of the floor, but as she would have put the satchel to one side, something impelled her to reach within it again and draw out another small bundle from among the parchments, instruments and the thin dry clutches of certain dried herbs and leaves. Nimue did not know what else was contained in the satchel apart from the crystal. But she was familiar enough with the ways of magic, and aware that when it was the right time and she was ready, she would be guided to whatever was best for her needs and purposes.

Now she unwrapped the second small bundle and found that she was looking at the painted cards Gereint Gwynne had shown her once, explaining to her that they could be used as a focus for the inner vision, to enable the enlightened to see true.

'But you are born a wise child, you do not need them,' he had said, smiling. Now, though, sitting alone with the cards in her hands, she remembered that he had added, so quietly that she had forgotten he had said it, the single word — 'yet.'

She had not been curious then, and she had forgotten the cards, until this moment. She turned one over, and saw the figure she had seen once in a vision where Pendragon's father, the old wizard, had passed on to her his blessing and his message for his son.

That fateful message concerning the legacy he had left, the words that spoke of gold hidden, gold within the earth somewhere to be found on Pendragon land.

There was an image of an aged man in the rough robe of a holy brother, a hermit such as the one who had married them — Pendragon and herself — in the little chapel at the shrine of Saint Mary above the frozen Elwy river, on the night of Christmas. Looking at it, Nimue felt as though there were other images crowded like phantoms beyond the painted card, but she did not want to examine them and biting her lip, she put it down and took the next.

It was a king, a worldly prince in his state, richly robed with orb and sceptre. Her throat contracted, for though this man was of advanced years, his beard long and grey, the king she saw was her husband, her dear scarred lord of dark and light, Pendragon, the man who in this world would always rule her heart. Her hands were trembling. The whole of her life — the whole of all life — seemed to be here.

As she fumbled in sudden clumsiness with the cards, one of them fell to the floor, and Nimue reached to pick it up. The picture was of a woman, heavily cloaked and veiled, with symbols in her hands and a moon above her head. Remote and unearthly, yet to Nimue, suddenly — inexplicably — there was menace. As she looked at the painted figure, the room seemed to darken as though the light outside the casement thickened and coiled upon itself.

She turned over another card.

It was another woman — young, with an embroidered gown and her hair dressed richly, flowing over her shoulders. She looked upwards, her face tilted sweetly, one arm lifted. She was holding up a bright star in her hand, and as Nimue gazed at it, it was as though the dark withdrew, slowly and reluctantly, so that the light of early evening once more filled the chamber with its watery greenish sheen, and she could hear the doves at their soft cooing in the yard.

Something stole gently across her troubled heart, and she felt stilled and at peace. The pain of her husband's loss, the upsetting and disconcerting reactions she had experienced in her encounter with Lady Ardua and particularly to the man whose uncomfortable powers she felt helpless to fathom — all these seemed distanced from her. Beyond them too, the tasks and responsibilities that had been placed unasked upon her shoulders, the secretive machinations of government, the dark threat of the Hand itself, what were they and their account in the greater scheme of things?

'It is enough to hold fast to the light,' her father had always taught her, but she had not realised the true and subtle wisdom of the simplicity of those words. Until now as, distracted by cares and concerns, grieved and wounded from loss and the hurt of human loving, she looked for a long time at the star, burning steadily in the woman's hand, and was strangely comforted.

5

Nimue had been more shaken than she had realised by the encounter in the Strand. She made no attempt to call on Ruffard Rowland — or anyone else — and told herself it was because the planet Mercury was in retrograde, and communication was not well-aspected. But the truth was that she had felt exposed, threatened, and was uneasily conscious that she needed to build up her reserves of power if she was to be able to challenge the dark magic — whatever it proved to be — behind the Hand.

Her father had many times emphasised that it was not enough to be born with the Sight, with the ability to use it. The powers were lent, not given, and the possessor must respect himself as a channel only for superior power, which it was his duty to keep as pure and unsullied by the tarnish of human passions as he could. This, Gereint Gwynne told Nimue, was the reason why all who trod the path of the spirit to God — whichever deity they perceived — must take time apart from the world to consciously cultivate their spiritual vision, to cleanse themselves of the inevitable dross of the earth and reaffirm their true existence as a part of the purity of the world beyond.

'Only the man who will never be more than a man will not recognise that he is, of himself, nothing,' Gereint said often, and more than ever before, Nimue was aware now of the need to go quietly apart, to distance herself and lift her thoughts to the light — 'to the star,' she thought, remembering the card that had brought her comfort.

She needed to gather her resources together and to examine what had happened and was about to happen — not so much in the world of the city and those who inhabited it, but within herself.

For she was no longer detached, unaffected by human passions. She had not wanted to listen to the low-voiced words of the Counsellor, it was true, and she was certain they were filled with hidden, probably sinister, meanings, yet they seemed to echo in her ears, even when she attempted to ignore them.

'You are stronger than you think — .'

Well, she trusted to God for her strength. But the rest of the sentence lingered with more ominousness — with an implied threat, she wondered dubiously?

'Weaker than others believe — .' She found it disturbing that the shadowed eyes of this man she did not, could not trust, seemed to be the only ones that could see the struggle within, her desperate attempt to cling to peace and the certainty that all was well when Pendragon had gone — .

★ ★ ★

Yet it was restful within the little house on the banks of the Thames. Though the city roared and smoked and she was a part of it, she had begun to feel that there was as much of a sanctuary within her own walls as there had ever been when her father had been alive, or within the quiet chamber in Pendragon tower — now gone for ever, since the fire — where she had sat and looked at the globe of the heavens, the firmament within, starry and bright, and Pendragon's eyes had met hers across it, and she had known that she had come home.

Nimue was conscious that though she had returned to London, she had changed and would never truly belong to the city again. She would never belong to any place in the future, for she carried the consciousness of her own destined place within her — as a Pendragon, one who must more than ever keep herself apart, and her vision clear. Her own best counsellor from now on, would always be herself.

So she went about her daily routine for the most part in silence, and since Huw could not speak and Math did not choose to speak, it was left to Mistress Grabbon, unaware of any spiritual stillness and unmoved by visions, to bring the bustle of the everyday to kitchen and parlour. She spoke to herself and to the absent Mister Grabbon at great length, and was often to be found conducting conversations with the empty air as she waddled lightly for all her pear-shaped bulk, from room to room. Sometimes Nimue thought that it was Mistress Grabbon who was the visionary and not herself or Huw. For what was magic after all but the language of faith and trust? And the good wife's faith and trust in her absent husband was absolute.

The world seemed far from the quiet house, and even Will, with his solid masculinity and physical presence, overlaid with the tinsel gossip and unreal realities, cock's blood and cheesecloth clouds of glory of the theatre, did not make an appearance. Nimue had a respite, and it was the sounds of the rain against the casement, the soft throaty murmuring of the doves and the far cries of the watermen that began to make up the shapes of her days.

She spent hours in her spiritual preparations, in prayer and meditation, for she realised now that the greater the gift of vision, the heavier the responsibility of the one who had been granted it. She had been a child, with a child's faith, that all would be well if she trusted in a higher power, that it would not fail her. But now she saw that faith alone was not enough. The power would never fail her, but she was only human clay, and she might fail herself.

Sometimes she thought she sensed her strength increase so that she was aware of shining presences with her, sharpening the sword she must wield for the light, at other times she despaired. But even as she gave herself up entirely to the will of that greater power, she was shown that there were realms beyond faith, beyond trust, and entered willingly into them. And in the stillness, it was though a blessing beyond anything she had ever imagined was placed gently and with infinite compassion upon her bowed head.

It was enough. Nimue realised intuitively — and with humble thankfulness — that she had passed this test, and that whatever the dark held, whatever the Hand signified, she could truly face it now. For though she died in the flesh, nothing could touch her immortal soul. That was in the hands of God.

* * *

And so, spiritually fortified, she sat in the parlour in the afternoon a week later, pondering on the worldly affairs she had so far avoided and anticipating her meeting with Robert Cecil the following day. Her workbox was beside her but she did not, like Mary Stoneyathe, amuse herself with would-be fine embroidery work. There was a shirt of Math's in Nimue's hands, and the household sewing waiting for her needle. It gleamed busily in her fingers, though her brow was puckered a little and her thoughts were far away.

She had prepared herself to confront whoever, or whatever she must, but since there had been no sign, no message, she began to consider whether she should make some more definite move herself in her undertaking to discover the Hand. She might further her supposed role as patroness of the arts, perhaps, and make her presence known by initiating cultural enquiries in the appropriate circles — or renew acquaintanceship with some of the magicians or cunning men who had, however casually, respected her father and his reputation.

Yet something — the fact that Mercury was retrograde? — held her back. She had no real idea of what to do, and the wise advice Gereint Gwynne would have given her, she knew, was in such a case, to do nothing. She began to anticipate that perhaps Robert Cecil, with the resources he had no doubt put into action since their meeting, would have some light to throw on the matter, some course of action in mind that she might follow.

But it was early the next morning, as she and Math were preparing to set out once again into the city, that the spark was set to the tinder — the sign she had been awaiting came, communication, for better or worse, was made. Huw came to summon her to the hall, for there was a messenger arrived, and an immediate answer required to the letter he carried.

Nimue took the parchment and broke the seal with a feeling of inevitability, somehow unsurprised, as though she had already lived through this moment.

Yet the contents of the letter were entirely unexpected.

She was informed by someone who signed herself Judith Carter, her 'dear sister in intent', that her company was eagerly desired on the following afternoon. Madam Carter, it appeared, was certain that she and Gereint Gwynne's daughter would not only be able to console each other in their mutual grief at his loss but would also find it beneficial to discuss their 'natural desire to see the world restored to its proper order'.

She would await Gereint's dear child, Madam Carter indicated, at the appointed hour at the house of 'my adherent Mister Jobling' in Chelsea, and the same Mister Jobling having willingly — nay, eagerly — offered the services of his coach and horses to ensure Nimue's comfort, she need only send word back with the messenger that she would come.

Madam Carter, a rather rambling correspondent, further hinted that there were 'matters of import' to be mentioned, 'such as only those possessors of above common talents might be aware.' She remained, she finished, Nimue's obedient servant and once again, 'sister in intent.'

The girl frowned over the letter, mystified. What connection could this garrulous gossip possibly have with the dark and sinister threat of the Hand of Glory? And yet her intuition told her the message was of the utmost significance — she could feel vibrations thrumming alarmingly from the parchment she held into her fingers, as though she was touching a deeply tolling bell. She read the words again, pausing over the signature.

Judith Carter? Nimue had no recollection of any Judith Carter, nor the slightest idea of what the woman meant by her heavily veiled insinuations regarding 'matters of import' of which 'only the possessors of above common talents might be aware'. And what of 'my adherent, Mister Jobling'? Shaking off the clinging threads of intrigue, Nimue looked up at the bearer of the message.

A sweating horseman in livery, an ordinary man carrying out the duties by which he honestly earned his board and his bread. Somehow, in the light of an April morning, it was difficult to believe that such person could possibly have any connections with plots, revolutions and dark magic.

'You serve Madam Carter?' Nimue said pleasantly, some instinct prompting her to add, with a smile: 'Though the livery, I suppose, is that of Mister Jobling.'

'Marm,' the messenger acknowledged formally — though unhelpfully — inclining his head. He had a harrassed air, he was young and distracted, and his fresh skin beneath sandy hair flushed at her directness. Nimue saw that he was unhappy in his role as messenger. In fact, she thought he was unhappy in general, at his whole situation. And there was an expression in his eyes that was somehow familiar, though she could not momentarily place it. Then she remembered — it was the same cloudy, doubtful unease that had flashed across Will's gaze when she spoke of the Hand and his fingers had lifted — then dropped again — towards the charm that hung at his neck.

Nimue was suddenly very still, very aware, and she paused for long moments, considering, even though she had her cloak around her, and Math was waiting at the gate in the walled garden, where honeysuckle grew in great masses across the worn stone, promising lushness and fragrance on summer evenings to come. She stood holding the letter, keeping the messenger waiting before her while she examined the thought that had so significantly presented itself.

Then: 'Perhaps,' she said pleasantly to the young man, 'you would like to go to the kitchen. Mistress Grabbon loves nothing better than to exchange a word with a personable gentleman and she will give you a cup of ale. You may return to your mistress and tell her that I will be happy to accept her invitation.'

As he responded with a slight, formal bow, she added as an afterthought: 'It is always pleasant to encounter the Hand — .'

But in the pause that followed, she saw that he had not taken any meaning from the word. Whatever he knew, or feared, or whatever it was that clouded the brightness of his eyes, it was not recognisable to him as an echo or rumour of the Hand of Glory.

'It is the hand of friendship to which I refer, of course,' Nimue smiled guilelessly. 'Pray inform your worthy mistress, sir, that I look forward with the greatest anticipation to our meeting.'

And indeed, as she and Math set out to the Strand she felt a stirring of more than just anticipation. So it had begun. Something had begun to happen, and her intuition told her she had, by whatever subtle or unexpected chance, been presented with a key that would unlock the mysteries guarding the true meaning and identity of the intelligence that was responsible for the threatening presence of the Hand.

She had sensed in the messenger's unease the same confusion, the same frustrated bafflement she had picked up in Will. There were double meanings — even, she thought, a kind of a grim humour — behind the image. And it was obvious now that nothing so crude as the hand severed from the wrist of a felon was involved here. No, she had been right to think the Hand of Glory was only a symbol. Whatever it represented, it was not the actual flesh of a dead man. But then, what?

It surprised her that the boy, the messenger had not been aware of that phrase, that meaningful term which provoked such reaction in others. Nimue wondered as she and Math proceeded on their way, what it was that had caused such disquiet in him — .

She had forgotten, for the moment, her forthcoming meeting with Robert Cecil. She was lost in speculation, completely unaware, her thoughts with the unknown Madam Judith Carter and 'my adherent, Mister Jobling'. Who were they? And what was their connection — with her, with each other, and perhaps most significantly, with the relationship they had so uncompromisingly claimed with Gereint Gwynne's memory? The messenger had of course not answered any of these questions for her. But he had been disquieted. Uneasy. With this she had to be, for the moment, satisfied.

★ ★ ★

The weather had changed dramatically, and they found the journey was pleasant in the morning which was not this day awash with rain but promisingly fresh with a blue sky and small fleecy white puffs of cloud sailing across the rooftops of the city. The spires of churches glittered in the light of a spring sun. There was a stirring of lightness and colour after so many weeks when it had seemed that the spring would never come. Evidence of the wet was everywhere still, dripping, glittering, but somehow the larks in the clear air lifted the soul as the newly-turned cloaks and smiles of the citizens going about their business lifted the spirits.

On this morning, Nimue did not regret the mysterious ridges of mountains crouching in the west and the shadows of the great oaks and tangled blackthorn making the Welsh hills places of sacred presence, silent with meaning. The great stone that spoke of ancient rituals, which watched above Gilbert Stoneyathe's manor of Grannah, where Nimue had stood in the dawn light when she had seen the last, the final vision of her husband riding towards her out of the sunrise, still held its own significance, its own meaning in her life. But it would always be there, always with the unspoken teachings of wisdom for the pupil who so earnestly strove to tread the path of high learning. Today Nimue found she was just a girl again.

She exclaimed, laughing with Math, at the antics of the crowds and the street criers, the colour and magnificence of those who jostled elbow to elbow in what must surely be the greatest of cities. The hawkers in Cheapside were figures of mystery with their oriental faces and yellow silken robes, selling such wonders as monkeys and live peacocks, jewels and spices from far Cathay and carpets from Ispahan. The gilded wares of the goldsmiths glittered as golden as the gingerbread men, fragrant with currents and freshly baked, hot from the oven, that the two of them bought, and which burned their fingers as they ate.

Somehow, on this morning when the sun shone as it had not shone for many a day over London, Nimue felt as though she had been given a gift of new youth and joy. One could not mourn for ever. There would be moments of awareness, sure, of her loss again, and harrowing spasms of longing. But life moved on. What was past was past. She would look neither forward nor backward. For today, she would take the moment as it came and leave all else to God.

She gave herself up to the pleasure of the morning, the sounds, sights and new-washed colours of a London stirring good-naturedly from a long and dogged season that had all but drowned it, and it was not until she and Math (surreptitiously licking the last traces of the gingerbread from their fingers in childish abandon) straightened themselves into dignity to present themselves at the apothecary's shop that Nimue's thoughts returned more soberly to graver matters. Mister Cecil and her mission, the letter she had just received. Madam Judith Carter. Mister Jobling of Chelsea.

'Do you know ought of them, sir?' she enquired of Robert Cecil as they sat together in the little room behind the apothecary's. She had told him immediately on her arrival of the letter and of her conviction that this was the expected approach to her in some way, however bizarre it appeared, from the Hand. She was, after all, being courted as her father's daughter, as a cunning woman of influence, a woman of power.

To her surprise, Mister Cecil's heavy brows shifted in what seemed like irritation.

'I wish I could share your optimism, madam,' he said dismissively. 'Yet I cannot think so. Judith Carter? She has long been known to us, a charlatan, a dabbler in the most dubious kind of hokus-pocus, yet shrewd enough, I grant you, so that she has never openly been accused of fraudulent dealings. Mister Jobling had best be wary. Madam Carter has married and buried two husbands, both of whom left her their not inconsiderable assets.' He made a slight, intolerant gesture. 'Oh, she will not claim openly that she can conjure with spirits, for this would take her to the courts, but there is no doubt that she encourages the credulous to creep to her secretly in the night for potions and philtres.'

Nimue was silent. This was the woman who claimed, at least by inference, to have been on some sort of intimacy with her father?

'Mister Jobling of Chelsea. Hmm,' went on Robert Cecil ruminatively. 'Well, there may perhaps be something there. The man has connections abroad, I believe, particularly with the Russias and the northern hemispheres. He is a furrier by trade, of some wealth, mistress, though he has political leanings, and has been noted as consorting with dissidents and known rabble-rousers.' He turned the pomander ball that hung round his neck on a gold chain thoughtfully in his fingers, lifting it to his nose so that he could smell the sharp clove scent.

'I suppose this is what might have

been expected,' he said distastefully, as Nimue remained silent, considering his words. 'Your father — and indeed, your husband's family also — commanded respect for their learning I understand. Their reputations were based on wise philosophies and the sciences — astronomy, alchemy, recognised spheres of activity, rather than the doubtful conjuring of witchcraft.' He gave a slight shrug. 'But these cunning women like Judith Carter — they deal in pettiness, spite and the cultivation of fear and amazement in simple minds. I personally, Mistress Pendragon, am of the opinion that taking notice of such people plays into their hands, and bestows upon them an illusion of power they do not possess.'

Nimue regarded him with interest, surprised at his sudden eloquence. There was heightened colour in his heavy features, and a kind of restrained anger brightening his eyes. She had not suspected that Robert Cecil possessed such passion.

'Take the case of Mother Samwell, who selfishly persisted in dragging her husband and her daughter with her to the gibbet only last year,' Robert Cecil was proceeding, as though impelled to pursue his argument. 'Such as she, they bring about their own misfortune and will condemn themselves out of their own mouths. The woman was patently no more a witch than any other, yet in her arrogant foolishness she would not be advised, and through her stubbornness brought about not only her own end but that of her man and her child.' He gave a contemptuous half-laugh that had no mirth in it.

'Oh, I have no fear of witches, mistress. My soul is promised salvation and no woman can alter that.'

Ah, Nimue thought, so that was it. She was extremely interested in this unintentional revelation by Robert Cecil of the defenses he felt it necessary to employ to protect himself against the influence of that most deadly of creatures — woman. Yet there was unexpected logic here and unwilling good sense, even generosity and tolerance. Nimue began, for the first time, to feel some liking for this man.

'Madam Carter does not appear to have brought about her end, rather to have created a better life for herself,' she pointed out mildly, and Robert Cecil's fist curled with controlled violence round the jewel in his fingers.

'If you choose to respond to this — ah, invitation — you will meet her, Mistress Pendragon, and must form your own judgement,' he said repressively. 'I am not here to condemn her or argue her case. But for certain, this woman, like others of her kind, is no threat except to the simple-minded who see wonders everywhere because they are told to do so. It is obvious that she sees the opportunity to trade on an assumed familiarity with men of repute such as your father, and seize on his good name, grasping the reputation of others as these creatures do. You say you do not remember her?'

'I have never heard of her, sir,' Nimue said quietly. 'And I am sure my father would have had no dealings with her either, if she is as you describe. He might at some time have spoken to her — counselled her — ,' she added doubtfully, thinking of Jemima Blackcross, who had been a similar sort of woman.

'It is just as I thought,' Robert Cecil said, frowning. 'She will make claims your father cannot repudiate, being now deceased. I advise you to bear in mind what I have told you, Mistress Pendragon. You are young and unused to the deviousness of such females,' he added with unexpected tolerance.

'Thank you, sir,' Nimue responded composedly, though she smiled a little to herself. In spite of his dismissive attitude, she had every intention of taking the invitation seriously when she called upon Judith Carter. And Mister Jobling. Tomorrow. For a moment's consideration had been more than long enough to wipe away any trace of a smile. Had it been only the reputation of a scheming cunning woman which had caused the expression of wariness in the young courier's eyes, the same that had been in Will's? On the whole, with a fresh stirring of expectancy, she thought not.

Robert Cecil was speaking again, turning the subject to Ireland.

'Your — ah — information concerning the western coast, the Cliffs and the Bay you mentioned — they are being exhaustively investigated. They may prove particularly significant since they do not lie within the territories of the lady Grainne's ancient clan, the O'Malleys, in Connaught.' He gave a thin smile. 'The — ah — gentleman you observed at the Earl of Ormond's gathering is following up the lead you have given us with the Irish community in London and I can assure you that if there is anything to be discovered there regarding this particular concern — and the lady's supposed recognition of yourself, madam — he will find it. My father especially commends your suggestion that the Hand of Glory is merely a cypher, a symbol and does not signify some ordinary threat such as might be expected. He requests your further thoughts on the matter, if you have any to give him.'

Nimue hesitated only a moment.

'There is a man,' she said. 'I have seen him twice, once when Will Shakespeare, the actor who was my father's friend, took me to a tavern, and the second time here in the Strand when I left you two weeks ago, Mister Cecil. They call him the Counsellor, the Holy Devil, and he is companioned by a lady of eccentric appearance, the Lady Ardua. Perhaps you have some knowledge of them.'

She paused, but Robert Cecil, carelessly twisting his pomander chain, did not look at her.

'Well — and what of him, this man?'

Nimue, confused, made a small

movement with her hand.

'I do not know, sir, he may be a religious, his words would suggest that he advocates some gospel of counselling and comfort, but I am not sure. He has power beyond the ordinary, and it may be that it is he, with his will and intent, who blocks the vision of the Hand — .'

To her surprise — and a slight, cold shock at the unexpectedness of it — Robert Cecil interrupted her, his manner impatient, almost contemptuous.

'And can you tell me no more than this, that 'it may be', woman? What is your own power if it can be spelled by the rantings of a common street preacher? Did your father not instruct you in philosophies beyond superstition and terror of threatened damnation?'

She was shaken out of her complacency.

'I am sorry, sir. It was not damnation that this man promised me, rather — .' Her voice faltered. She heard again the low, almost whispered words: ' — out of darkness into the light — wipe away your tears — I will console you and comfort you — .'

'He is dangerous, sir,' she said with conviction, swallowing the ache of loss and longing that had made her vulnerable. 'Of that I am certain.'

Robert Cecil stared at her for so long that she felt colour begin to stain her cheeks.

'The man has a fascination for women, sure, a way with him,' he shrugged at last. 'Yet he is harmless enough.'

Nimue's chin lifted, though her face burned at his casual words.

'Pardon me, Mister Cecil,' she said quietly. 'My father taught me to be aware of the powers, but they are neither harmless or harmful, neither good nor bad in themselves. It is how they are employed which determines whether good or evil may follow their use. And I tell you again, this man has great power.'

But Robert Cecil's reaction was as

inexplicable as his outburst had been. He continued to stare at Nimue, but she did not think he had been listening to her words. Then he said loudly:

'The Lady Ardua is of gentle birth, for all her peculiarities. She is a true aristocrat.'

'He knows her,' Nimue thought with surprised conviction, and her mind added incredulously: 'Knows her *well*. And — loves her?'

This unexpected turn of events, and Robert Cecil's brusqueness — equally inexplicable — held her silent. After a moment, he turned from her as though he had been caught out in some indiscretion, and busied himself ostentatiously with some parchments that lay on the table beside him. Nimue watched him, considering.

Yes, though he obviously had no intention of taking her into his confidence, he was on very familiar terms with the lady, so much so that he had felt it necessary to defend her reputation even though Nimue had not actually made any criticism of her at all. His instincts had sprung to protect her, perhaps not against accusations of treason or sinister dealings, but against any suggestion that she might appear ridiculous. It was curiously endearing, and the first sign this rather shallow man had shown that he was capable of any attachment at all to a female. Nimue would have liked to question him further, but she realised it would be unwise. No doubt all these subtleties of intrigue would be revealed to her in time — but in the meanwhile, she had a distinct impression that she had been dismissed.

She waited for a little longer then as he made no move to address her further, she rose composedly.

'I think there is no more I can usefully add sir. With your permission, I will leave you.'

'Do so, by all means, Mistress Pendragon,' Robert Cecil agreed rather awkwardly, adding in a non-committal tone: 'You may send a message here requesting Dragon's Head — the term the apothecary will recognise — if you wish to contact me again. Though I doubt,' he added after a short pause, 'that Madam Carter or Mister Jobling will pose any threat to the peace of the kingdom, and as for the man, this Counsellor, you may rest assured, he is of no account. Save only to credulous females,' he finished pointedly, not looking at her.

Nimue felt the colour rise once again in her cheeks, though she was certain he had not meant the words to be insulting. His attention was elsewhere — no doubt on the suspected slight which she had not intended, towards the Lady Ardua — but as she was about to leave through the curtained arras, he appeared to recollect himself and recalled her.

'My father — Lord Burleigh — bids me advise you, Mistress Pendragon, that the documents of the legalities regarding your property have been placed in the hands of a lawyer in your name, and will require your attendance without delay, in order that the formalities of the matter may be settled.'

'My — property — ?' Nimue repeated, startled.

'Her Majesty's gift, your house and land. The relevant documents have been lodged with Mister Ruffard Rowland, a lawyer highly recommended to you by my father, and one who is, he assures you, competent to advise you most sagaciously concerning the affairs of your late husband's estate in Wales.' There was an expression on Robert Cecil's face now that Nimue could not identify. Secrecy? Smug superiority? When she did not reply, he added with some impatience:

'Mister Rowland's house is situated — .'

'Thank you, sir,' Nimue interrupted coolly, recovering her poise. 'I am familiar with the name of Mister Rowland, and know where he lives. Please thank my Lord Burleigh for his concern of me, and assure him I will

170

attend to the matters he mentions as soon as I may.'

Robert Cecil inclined his head, and Nimue bade him goodday and left the apothecary's shop with Math, who as usual seemed to materialise from nowhere. She was in a state of bafflement. Apart from the question of his relationship — whatever it was — with Lady Ardua, she was convinced Robert Cecil was also keeping other information from her. Something that appeared to cause him a kind of grim amusement — or had she mistaken his expression as he watched her go?

And it was surely more than chance that she had been directed to the lawyer Ruffard Rowland. She had not mentioned him to Burleigh — nor indeed to anyone. Nobody knew of her visit to his house except Math, who had been with her — and the man himself — .

6

The coach which arrived to transport Nimue to Chelsea the next afternoon was luxurious, even ostentatious. She seated herself within it and leaned back against the seat thoughtfully, as it commenced its jolting. Once again the day was fair, filled with promise, but though glad of the freshening breeze and the sudden blooming of greenery beneath a few days of sunshine, she was once more oblivious to the scene outside. Her attention was turned within, and had been since her meeting the previous day with Robert Cecil.

She had taken the opportunity to call immediately afterwards at the house of the lawyer, Ruffard Rowland, only to find that he was absent on business, and had had to content herself with a message requesting him to visit her when he returned, which she was told by the goodwife who, spotless in white linen cap and apron, beamingly answered her knock, might not be for some days. However, Nimue was in a way relieved at the delay, for she felt time was needed to try and sort out the threads that had begun to reveal themselves in a tangled skein to her, and try to make sense of the pattern they represented.

Though she had pondered on Mister Cecil's repeated assurance that she could dismiss her suspicions of the 'Counsellor', she could not accept his judgement on the matter. She knew she would be foolish to ignore the promptings of her own inner awareness, though she had not yet been able to decide what her true feelings were towards the man, whether the power he held in check was merely a disconcerting ability to breach her own emotional defences or a threat of more sinister import, something that might need to be formally confronted in the service for which Burleigh had appointed her.

But if Robert Cecil was acquainted with the Lady Ardua — if, as she was convinced, he knew the eccentric gentlewoman well and felt some fondness towards her but for some reason known only to himself, was not prepared to admit it — then it was possible that he was deliberately allowing himself to be deluded with regard to Lady Ardua's activities and those of her supposedly pious friend. Yet Nimue knew Robert Cecil was a skilled and experienced servant of the state. Was it likely that he would make such careless and over-emotional errors of judgement?

On her return home, she had sought the quiet of her chamber to consult her father's crystal, but her own increasing uneasiness — largely, if she was honest with herself, concerning the man in the dark cloak — blocked her vision, and she could gain only fragments. There were undoubtedly facts she was unaware of, and she tried to clarify her impressions by once more looking at the painted cards which had brought her comfort and reassurance when she had seen the image of the young woman holding the star.

But this time, the card she took seemed to vibrate with urgency and warning. There was a man standing in a moving chariot, while the team of horses harnessed to it galloped ahead seemingly uncontrollably, as though he could not check them. Nimue felt her breath catch in her throat, as though it was herself in the chariot, speeding to some unknown, perhaps hazardous, fate. But into the mist of panic, she seemed to feel her father's reassuring hand on her own, as it held the card, and his voice, unemotional, yet infinitely calming to her.

'Go with the flow of the stream, Nimue, do not try to fight the current that takes you to your destiny. Only be watchful. Seize the chance as it comes. Trust in yourself. And remember — .'

It was as though he was beside her, his eyes suddenly dissolving from gravity into humour, giving his deep, infectious chuckle. 'Power can take many forms. A smile from Helen was enough to challenge two armies and set them at each other's throats. You too are a woman — is that not sufficient power for you?'

But it was the very fact that she was a woman which was at the root of her disquiet, she thought uneasily. If she had been a man, she would not have been so affected by the low words of the Counsellor, forming as they had done, their shapes of bewitchment in the rain. She would not find herself — as she did now — struggling to keep back her longing, her yearning for her dear lord, biting her lip against the tears. And feeling increasingly uneasy in the rising flood of her grief. For the strength of the Evil One lay, she knew, only in the advantage the dark might take over human frailty, its power only the power we give to it ourselves, and the opportunity we allow it to overshadow us.

Nimue pressed her clenched fist to her mouth, yet she had to admit the truth. She did not want to let go of the memories of her wedding to Pendragon, nor accept that the bridal night she had never yet spent in his arms could never come. It was true, that man — whatever he was — had seen into her heart, beyond the wise child with her wisdom and her awareness of the light, to the woman parted untimely from her mate, and his words had stirred up all the yearnings of human passion she was too weak to repress. But if he could do that — and so disarm her in a moment — how might she hope to confront him if it had to be so, if he was her enemy and the enemy of all that was good and stable in Elizabeth's England? Was the task she had undertaken to fail before she had attempted it?

★ ★ ★

When at last she slept that night, it was not to peaceful slumber from which she might wake refreshed, but to the awareness of another of the tangled threads that made up the pattern that confronted her. The symbol — the image — the Hand of Glory. She could perceive it, she could sense it with her intuition, but she could not as yet see its significance.

She found herself again on that far wild coast she had seen before, where the great Cliffs of Moher rose gigantically from the sea. She looked once more on the ocean beyond, the changing light over the grey-blue of the water, waiting, expectant. And this time, she saw it — a ship. A galleon, its sails like the folded wings of a bird, was standing off from the coast, wraithlike yet clinging to the sea, and from it she saw even as she watched, a small boat put out from it to make its way towards the land. A dark dot against that vast expanse — .

The scene, the moment, seemed

to intensify, to burn itself into her awareness. And then the dream blurred into fragments, and was gone. Only the sense of fatefulness, of destiny remained, and Nimue woke with a fastbeating heart and quickened breath. She sat up, momentarily unaware of her surroundings — grey sky, grey sea swirling — within the looped curtains of her bed to see the brightness of a new day lightening the casement, and hear the familiar sounds of the city recalling her from that wild ocean shore. She had the feeling — the conviction — that she knew something of immense import.

But in the name of heaven, what?

* * *

Lost in her thoughts, unaware, Nimue went mechanically about the morning's duties. No rain, not even a April shower this day, and she busied herself for a while in her garden, replenishing her store of herbs from the plot which Math — who had been instructed in such

179

matters by Pendragon himself — tended so lovingly that Nimue suspected the plants knew his voice and the touch of his fingers. Math's world lay beyond the temporal, it was not for nothing that Pendragon had chosen him as an apprentice in the spirit, but for all the clear light of his eyes, the boy was still young (so Nimue, in an assumption of maturity, told herself), too young to be able to enlighten her on the matters that were absorbing her attention.

She was convinced — especially since Grainne O'Malley had so unaccountably appeared to recognise her and connect her with the Irish land she had never seen — that her glimpses of the wild western seacoast were no ordinary dreams. Her father had spoken sometimes of magicians and cunning men who claimed they could leave their bodies and travel by sorcery to other places. Could she, perhaps, have done so while she slept, without awareness?

Nimue recalled the sending of her

husband that had come to her out of the sunrise — something born of his love and care for her, though the ignorant might cross themselves and whisper of demons that took on familiar form. Could it be, even, that she had unknowingly, in the way of the old religion which the Pendragons had followed, it seemed, since ancient times, shape-shifted into some other body that was not her own? Yet if it was so, how had the Irishwoman been able to recognise her?

Yet the girl was certain she had not dreamed those cliffs that hung between sky and sea, pointing the way into infinity. She had, by whatever means, stood upon them and watched the boat put off from the ship that drifted in the grey mist of the horizon, like a bird at brief rest on the waves.

She was familiar with magic. Anything, however unlikely, was possible. Even Will Shakespeare, who was no dabbler in such things, was often heard to declare uncompromisingly to those who would argue the case that there were more things in heaven and earth than were dreamed of in their philosophy. He would discourse with Gereint Gwynne, allowing the older man to push back the boundaries of reality, intellectually and rationally. Until his poetic fancy was stirred, and then the laughter sparked in his eyes and the intellectual exercise became coloured with hyperbole.

He had said once in passing that actors were such troublesome creatures that he thought he would people his stage with fairies and elves.

'Sure, they are air, they will not remain within the confines of your 'little O', Will,' Nimue had teased, but Will's sweeping gesture defied prosaic reason.

'I will cast as many figures as Simon Forman, there is magic in my words, girl. I will cajole the Puck, to bewitch those who watch with their mouths open, and he will pass among them invisible, for what is it to him, who can put a girdle round the earth in an eye-blink?'

'Your spells will outlast those of all the sorcerers in London, Will,' Gereint Gwynne had said, and he was no longer smiling. He was gazing into the far distance, and there was something in his face that touched Nimue's senses coldly. Will must have felt it too, for he shivered.

'I thought of Kit,' he said, his mood suddenly sombre, when Gereint bade him put another log upon the fire. 'To outlast the sorcerers he would have traded with all the unseen kingdoms of goblin and ghoul, save that he was not satisfied with fairy dealings and like his own Faustus, who brings the groundlings to their knees to plead for his soul, Kit would dare to sup with the devil himself. A demon drove him, they said when he died.'

'No.'

There was authority in Gereint Gwynne's voice, and compassion. Nimue too thought of Will's friend Kit

Marlowe, fated and doomed as she had seen herself when she had met the young playwright with Will. She had said nothing, fearing her vision played her false, but only months later — the year before her father had gone — Kit had been stabbed to death, needlessly, uselessly, in a tavern brawl, his bright star blotted out, his voice screaming across the cosmos into oblivion, his very death an affirmation of life.

'His genius rode him, only. Yet he had not your detachment and sense of balance, Will. Life was his torment — he is resting now,' Gereint said quietly, and Will crossed himself. Outside, the voice of the Bellman broke the sudden stillness that had come over them.

'Remember the clocks,
Look well to your locks,
Fire and your light,
And God give you good night
For now the bell ringeth.'

There were three women in the long gallery of the house in Chelsea, with its mullioned casement windows that looked out onto the garden, but as Nimue paused on the threshold, the image that came to her mind was of some ancient group which dispersed and regrouped itself as unendingly as the shifting mist on a lonely moorland or seastrand. Surely she was looking at three witches — the three sisters of myth and timeless tale who spun the web of Wyrd, or the Fates who pursued man to his grave.

For a moment only the fancy was there, and then she saw that she knew two of them, they were quite real — perhaps disappointingly so — and in fact there were not three but four people present. The women were not alone. There was a man there too, richly dressed though too elderly and stout to play the gallant.

Light from the bright April afternoon played on the features of the three women, so that each had one side of her face in shadow. Nimue heard in the instant when she paused, before she went forward, the voices of Will and her father, one night when they had been speaking of evil, and the reality of evil in the world.

'To portray evil on the stage, man, I need the thunder-drum and the lightning bolt from heaven,' Will had argued, half-serious, half-laughing. 'The groundlings would not believe in it else. And when I create witches, they must be old hags, with cobwebby chins and bent backs. Toad and bat must attend them, and the sulphur that seeps from the cracks of the ceiling of hell must shroud their doings.'

'What of your contention that your art holds up a mirror to nature?' Gereint asked easily. 'Is it indeed so in the natural world?'

Will had shrugged.

'Is it the mirror that is evil, or what it reflects?'

'The nature of reality is what it appears to be?' Gereint countered, amused. Nimue had been listening in fascination, nodding in her corner as the fire sighed into hot red ashes in the hearth, weary of the late hour yet unwilling to leave them and go to her bed.

The conversations Will and her father conducted over their cups of ale held riches to rival the wealth of the Indies, often too deep for her young awareness. Will Shakespeare, youthful, gifted and feeling his way, would challenge the older man with his thoughts as a duelist might engage the blade of a master. Feint — pass — and then the lunge, to the heart. Yet it was Gereint whose blade flickered easiest, and whose point drew first and last blood.

Nimue had remembered this particular conversation because it had arisen after she and her father had witnessed the crowds at Southwark turning on the young widowed witch with her white swan-neck and her slim body heavy with a coming child; Gereint had taken in the distraught woman and her two young children, the boy clutching a small brindled cat with blood on its face fiercely to his chest, his eyes dark and impotent. After they had been comforted, and given food, drink and money, they had left the little house near London Bridge, and Nimue had never seen them again but she had not forgotten them.

The woman had been distraught with grief at the loss of her husband; bewildered at the fury of the mob. And it had been her pale beauty and the fact that she had been loved that had provoked the envy and spite of the less favoured, not any claim to secret power. Robert Cecil's contemptuous dismissal of sinister doings was based on true fact.

Yet: 'Evil must justify itself,' Gereint Gwynne had said, and Will puffed thoughtfully on the long stem of his tobacco pipe.

'But would they consider that, the prentices and scramblers in the pit? No, it must be more simple than that, man, they must have it spelled out for them. In the tradition of the theatre, each announces himself for what he is, on the side of the angels or not.'

'But do not the Greek dramatists teach that we must all work out our predestined doom, that it is not possible to defy our destiny?' Nimue had ventured from her corner beside the fire. 'There can be no choice between good and evil, if we must do what is laid down for us.'

The two men considered her words, and her father smiled.

'They call it *karma* in the East. She was born a wise child. What answer do you make to that, Will?'

'I say that my witches will appear in thunder, lightning and in rain, upon a blasted heath. And that they will prophesy and that man will choose and take his own destiny in his hands, yet all will come to pass as it was foretold,' Will stated, frowning into the flames. 'Evil is not some subtle concept, it is a choice made.'

'Even so, yet who would choose the evil way unless it seemed good to him?' queried Gereint, and Will laughed, shaking his head at his friend.

'Pax, pax! I am a poor craftsman with words, no scheming lawyer.'

'You will plead your case more cunningly than you know, for can a man govern the choice he will make? And by foreswearing evil, must he not first create his own devil to tempt him and thus give form and meaning to it?'

★ ★ ★

Somehow, although she had hardly known what to expect, and the message she had received had mentioned only the name of Judith Carter, Nimue was unsurprised. It was as if she had always known they would be here, the three of them, waiting for her. Strangers, yet she identified them with a sensation of complete familiarity.

Rosalind Blackcross, intense in dark

green velvet that set off her pale skin and the glitter of her eyes; and beside her, the severely-coifed holy sister (or whatever she professed to be) whom Nimue had met briefly at 'the Black's'. Maire Maeve of — where had it been? The third, she supposed, must be Judith Carter herself. A flamboyantly attired figure in slashed crimson, trimmed with laces and pearls.

They were three women such as she might encounter anywhere in the city, and yet when Nimue looked towards them, she saw Will's blasted heath, and three crones with their cobwebby chins and bent backs standing in the rain as thunder and lightning played about them. Then the woman in red stepped forward to greet her.

'Madam Pendragon, welcome,' intoned Judith Carter in a breathless contralto, and she held out one hand, making a gesture Nimue did not recognise before she added in a throaty murmur that was unexpectedly intense, 'Lady and mistress.'

'Do not look so surprised to see me. This was my doing — and you see, I was right, you needed my introduction.' Rosalind was smiling easily — almost Nimue thought, insolently — as she moved from the half-shadow into the light from the casement. Pale watery sunlight laid its gilt touch on the hair beneath her cap, and her outlined profile. Her eyes were alight, and in them an expression that resembled triumph. Only the third woman did not speak. She stood aloof, regarding Nimue from beneath the coif that shaded her face.

That there was indeed something meaningful, almost ritualistic in this meeting, the girl could not doubt. And she was glad, in however irrational a manner, that she had prepared herself for whatever it was that she might encounter. For there was a presence here in the gallery, something formless yet with the clinging miasma of a foggy cloud, threatening and chilling her, stifling the breath in her throat, dulling the spark of life in her soul.

Yet, could it be so? She looked again at the scene — and the figures — before her, chiding herself for irrational fancies. Three women — .

She might have been prepared to dismiss Judith Carter — on a sure instinct — as a domineering woman who loved her fleshly comforts and who had squandered her natural gift for the spiritual in the pursuit of earthly pleasure, the sort of person she had many times encountered in the past; and she was forced to admit she did not like Rosalind Blackcross. She considered the girl, if she was honest with herself, as too ambitious for position and power, using her inherited vision from her mother to further her own ends — but she was young, and would no doubt acquire true wisdom in time. As for the third woman, the one in the coif and grey robe, Nimue might hardly have noticed her except as a still presence.

But as they stood together, they

formed a meaningful group that was alien to the gallery where formal portraits stiffly observed the scene of domestic comfort — even luxury — from their opulent frames. Even more incongruous was the figure of the man (presumably Mister Jobling, the dealer in furs, owner of all this magnificence) which hovered rather diffidently at a distance, ruddy and lumbering in too-ornate black velvet trimmed with pearls. Nimue began to realise that despite the homely surroundings, she was facing an immense concentration of power, though it struck her as too heightened, too filled with human emotion to be truly of the spirit. She was aware, with a leap of her heart against the bodice of her gown, that she was in the presence of a sisterhood of magic, a triumvirate of sorceresses.

And then Rosalind Blackcross was speaking, drawing the young woman into the group with her voice. Though the woman in red had come forward to greet her, Nimue noticed vaguely, without being aware of it that none of them reached out to touch her.

'You know how it was that we two came to be friends,' Rosalind said familiarly, and though her voice was soft, it seemed to grate on Nimue as if a long finger-nail had been scratched across a piece of silk. There was an assumption of intimacy here that she found distasteful, for Rosalind was no more her friend than the many others who had come, unbidden, to seek out Gereint Gwynne at the house near London Bridge for his counsel and wisdom before they disappeared again into the busy, shifting antheap of the city. But Rosalind continued unperturbed: 'You have met our sister, Maire Maeve. And Dame Carter — .' She turned and gestured briefly. 'Dame Carter has long desired to make your acquaintance.'

'Indeed, lady, I have always held your father in the greatest veneration,' said the woman in red. Her eyes and her hair were very black, and Nimue could not help suspecting that though she must have been born with the eyes (perhaps, though, she used belladonna to darken them) her long tresses owed something to artifice. The result, though, was striking and hypnotic. She lifted her head and her hands in a pose that seemed deliberately studied for effect as she went on:

'Ah, he was a magus, a master. I longed to serve one of such stature, such authority. I asked him once — I offered my services as priestess — .' For a moment she paused, then her hands fell. 'But it was not to be.' Nimue was conscious of the piercingly intent gaze that seemed to touch her face as though fingers moved, groping, over her skin. Then the woman smiled with a dark, glittering brilliance.

'Yet he did not entirely abandon us. He sent his successor to us in a form even more powerful than those of Monachiel, Achides and Delgaliel, for is she not Athorebalo, Aeoou, Gaia, o Ma.'

Behind her breathless words, Nimue seemed to hear Pendragon's voice suddenly, as she had first heard it on the sea-strand when she had encountered his white horse Taliesin, fetlock deep in the moonlit waves, its rider a dark shadow rising from them dripping silver and calling on the spirits in a manner that might have brought the dead to life, if it had not been that he was simply expressing his frustration at so human an accident as a fall from his mount. Yet she could hear the words, words her father had sometimes used, though not often, for it was forbidden to conjure spirits and also, Gereint Gwynne had told Nimue that most things would be better left without the intervention of the forces favoured by other practitioners like John Dee.

'Raziel, Uriel, Azrael — .'

Her father had sometimes worked with magic, but he had not instructed Nimue. When the time came for her to summon the spirits, he had always told her, then she would know of it.

Now she saw with her inner vision that Judith Carter was a hysteric — and yet sometimes such loosening of the earthly restraints were necessary to ease the passage between the worlds, for the spirit to pass in and out of other realms. Her father had told her of many seemingly possessed by the epilepsy, who in their fits had seen with other eyes and been blessed with wisdom.

But there was something else, some ancient atavistic power in Judith Carter's words which held Nimue fixed by a sensation between awe and fear. As well as a growing awareness of the ridiculousness of the situation which she was sure Gereint Gwynne and Pendragon, if they had been present, would have found in a grim way, highly amusing. She had been prepared to risk her soul in her mission to find and overcome the Hand — but she had hardly expected to be confronted by a focussing of possible demonaic energies in the gallery of the house of a plump, red-faced furrier in Chelsea.

Even as these thoughts whirled at speed through her mind, however, she recollected, as her father had known only too well, that there was no right or official place to discover magic. It existed everywhere, behind and beyond the shapes of all familiar things, ever present to those who would seek it.

So she drew a breath, willing herself to confront the presence she sensed in the gallery — something that filled the air, smothering her and dulling her senses — something that hovered, unseen, yet in a moment might make itself visible — .

And then, into the tight, intense core of the moment, there was a movement. A little dog ran forward, its large eyes hidden beneath a thick mop of hair. It went to Judith Carter's feet and bowed itself on all its four paws before her red velvet shoes, putting its forepaws together as though it was praying. Then it rolled upon the floor waiting to be petted, and the spell — whatever it had been — was broken. The gallery clarified itself into focus, filled only with sunlight, and Judith Carter bent to her familiar, crooning love-words to it.

The tension was broken, and Nimue wondered dazedly, groping for her poise, whether it had been there at all. The three women were just three women again, foolish as only women can be over their animals. She blinked her eyes, shaking away the veils that still clung.

'I have not been blessed with children, and this is my substitute,' Judith Carter said, smiling in a quickly altered mood of doting fondness as she swept the little creature up into her arms. 'He was brought for me from the land of China, and he has a lion's heart.'

She spoke with the candour of a large and overgrown child, and as Nimue caught Rosalind Blackcross's eye, the other young woman lifted her brows in tolerant amusement.

'This is not what you expected, perhaps. You are surprised to see me, to see us. But we thought it was better this way.'

'Better?' But even as Nimue voiced the query, the third member of the group moved forward with the noiseless, gliding step of the holy nun.

'Failte, mo dreirfuir,' she murmured, her voice low. 'Welcome sister. We have been waiting for you.'

* * *

Why had she thought this woman colourless, of no account? As she looked into the pale eyes below the coif, Nimue was aware of a strength that was disciplined and controlled, a mature spirit far beyond the trivialities of lap dogs and the cares of foolish women. The eyes measured her, assessed her, and Nimue felt her colour rising. Then the woman spoke again.

'It has been a long search, my sister, and I am thinking you are weary. Come and sit with us, and we will speak of how we can help you.'

There was a note in her voice that seemed to touch Nimue's inmost heart, the place where the pain and turmoil of her husband's loss still wove their dark webs in patterns of anguish. Nimue felt disarmed, open to this woman's perception and the tears pricked suddenly behind her eyes.

'Help me?' she said helplessly, and Maire Maeve gave a little smile.

'Your father was a great magus, I am thinking, but he was only a man. And you, after all, are only a woman, young, touched by tragedy. You are perhaps unaware of your power. We will help you to discover yourself.'

She reached out one hand and as though impelled, Nimue lifted her own to take it. But before she could do so, she seemed to hear a voice ringing in her ears, as though from a far distance, and she hesitated as she tried to grasp the words. They came through time and space, mingled with the hoarse shriekings of seabirds — or the souls of drowned mariners — and the suck and swell of the sea.

'*Santa — Santa Catalina — .*'

She must have spoken them aloud, for she became aware when her vision cleared that Maire Maeve was staring at her, hand fluttering at her breast as though she crossed herself. 'It is inspired she is, and upon the holy saints that she calls,' she declared, her pale eyes gleaming with fervid fire as she turned to Rosalind and Judith Carter. Then she turned back to Nimue. 'Sister, more than you know, you have the gift of truth. Sit, and we will speak of how we can help each other.'

7

The colours of spring were suddenly, dramatically, blazing everywhere. There were blossoms tossing on the fruit trees, overnight it seemed, froths of pink and white waxen petals joyous and liberal with their scent. The gardens of the city overflowed, birds sang, and the world woke to a new awareness of the joy of living. In the courtyard of the little house beside the Thames, the doves fluttered their feathers in the sunlight, calling to each other, seeming to parade their finery in the same way the good citizens of London were opportunely making haste to walk abroad in celebration of the somewhat delayed advent of the spring, season of mirth and madness.

This morning, Mistress Grabbon's melodious phrases in the kitchen were echoed by the strains of lute and virginals from the parlour, where the casement was flung wide. Will Shakespeare, lounging easily beside Nimue, had brought his instrument and plucked the strings, his face an actor's mask that cameleon-like, switched from joy to woe, as he sang his latest songs for the girl's pleasure.

Most of the songs Will wrote for his plays were given to his Fools — who, Gereint Gwynne had commented, were generally the wisest men of all.

'For the Fool acknowledges his folly,' he said lightly, 'while the wise man never considers but that he is wise.'

Nimue loved the paradoxes, the double-edged expressions of wit and wisdom that were Will's trademark, and listened entranced as his mellow baritone warbled of love before it dirged death like the tolling of a far-off, warning bell. The morning was vivid with new life, with the reaffirming it seemed of hope that had been long abandoned.

The theatres, he assured her suddenly,

breaking off with a discord, would surely be allowed to open again soon, for this bright day came as the forerunner of better times. The threat of the plague was receding, people were tired of tragedy and sickness and death. Will, ever the optimist, detailed the latest news of the company, of the city gossip, and of more immediate concern to himself. He was doing well, the future was promising, he was a man of business now, and their company would go from strength to strength. He was going to buy a fine new house and Anne and the children could take their places as dependents of a prosperous, rising man of the world.

Nimue was glad to hear such domestic gossip, and the details of Will's newest idea for a play, how the Burbages were planning to counter their competition from Edward Alleyne of the Rose — Richard Burbage, Will declared, had not yet reached his true strength as a tragedian, and he had in mind some sweeping, dramatic representation of a new kind of hero, a man who would possess a fatal weakness, one flaw in an otherwise heroic nature, which would bring about his downfall, not as the Greeks had taught, *hubris*, the pride that challenged the gods. In the parts he intended to create, Rich would achieve new heights, and set their kind of theatre in a starry firmament of its own — something that would more than eclipse the latest fashion of Boy Players whose popular success threatened to capture their audiences.

A new playhouse was being considered, he told her. Across the river, on Bankside, hopefully to compete with the Rose. The theatre would boom after the years of restrictions imposed by the plague, and the people wanted escape after too close contact with death.

'You too, need to laugh again, girl,' he told Nimue, looking sideways at her slim, grave figure at the virginals. She could play a little, enough to carry a tune, and had been happy to find the instrument included in the furnishings of her house, for music, Gereint Gwynne had always maintained, was one of God's greatest blessings to mankind, a gift free to all.

'For do we not, as the birds, possess each a voice with which to give thanks to our maker?' he would ask, and he told Nimue — on one of the rare occasions he spoke of the girl's mother — that she had had the Welsh love of song and the tongue of a skylark. Nimue was aware that she had not inherited this gift to any marked degree, but she loved music and the making of it.

This morning, following her visit to Chelsea, she was more grateful than ever of the chance to sit and idle in Will's company, glad to be able to lose herself for a while in gossip and chatter, touching the keys of the virginals and singing songs that concerned themselves with love-frolics beneath the greenwood tree, or overly-dramatic protestations of imminent decease from a broken heart at love's distain. She was relieved to feel the press of everyday, trivial things around her, for the previous day had taken her too close to matters which were not of the everyday, but were of other worlds not of her own choosing, ominous and hazardous.

The implications, the subtleties of that meeting in the gallery at Chelsea had yet, she thought with increasing apprehension, to reveal themselves fully. She was not even certain of her own perceptions, her own judgement, for she had woken filled with self-doubts. Had it been mere arrogance to think she, in her inexperience, might challenge the might of the Hand? This first confrontation with its power, even at a distance, had left her shaken and badly disorientated.

★ ★ ★

For it had been as she had thought — and yet nothing she might have imagined. She had been right to trust her intuition, the prompting of her inner voice — and yet it seemed she had also been mistaken. Was her vision, then, failing her? For it appeared she had made grave errors — and her attempts to interpret the situation had been far from accurate.

It was true that she had been approached because of her powers, her influence, and because she was her father's daughter — yet she had been sought not to join with the dark magic that hid its face behind the symbolism of the Hand of Glory, but to confront it and overthrow its influence. Moreover, she felt helplessly that she had lost her detachment, her ability not to let her emotions rule her. For the meeting, far from reassuring her that she was not alone, had made her feel more isolated than ever.

Who were these women who claimed to be her sisters in magic and intent? Rosalind Blackcross, Judith Carter and Maire Maeve — three powerful personalities from very different back-grounds, from three points of the compass, they had converged. Three sorceresses who, united in their awareness of the threat that hung over the kingdom, had pledged to dedicate themselves and their considerable abilities, (Nimue gathered from the information they cautiously vouchsafed her), to challenge and destroy it. And, in the awareness of the work she had done in the past with her father — also, seemingly, aware of the reputation of the Pendragons — they were desirous to include her in their number, both for her father's sake and for her own.

It appeared, on the surface, that events were working in her favour. She had not only begun to make headway in the task the Queen had assigned her, to discover the nature of the Hand, but she seemed to have gained powerful allies — allies, moreover, who apparently knew more about the threat and what it portended than any of the officials of the crown. And yet, Nimue was still floundering, for her meeting with the three women had told her nothing. It had largely been conducted (as many consultations involving magic and spiritual matters often had to be because of their ephemeral nature), in riddles and images.

She had to admit that this was not really to be wondered at, for the wise needed to protect their wisdom. Crass mentalities of ignorance and superstition were easily alarmed, provoked to violent reaction born of fear, for they could not comprehend the truth, and viewed it as a threat rather than an enlightenment. Yet she had been surprised — and a little wary — to be treated with such over-zealous carefulness herself. Did they not trust her enough to speak plainly? If they had held her father in such high esteem as they claimed and even sought to include her as one of their immediate circle, there was no necessity for subterfuge. The language of the truth should be simple and direct, and Gereint Gwynne had taught his daughter not only to see clear but to speak without guile.

Each of the women in the gallery had her own particularly strong and well-defined characteristic, representing a different branch of the spiritual. Judith Carter, Nimue felt, was inclined to dramatise. She seemed to be under the impression that Nimue was a member of the same Druidic priesthood to which the old wizard Pendragon had apparently belonged. Or at least, some kind of pagan hierarchy, of which Judith Carter herself was by her own admission a priestess. And Maire Maeve, in her severe robe and coif, was surely of one of the strictest Orders of sisterhood, her whole attitude spoke of great discipline and asceticism. Rosalind, the youngest of them all, had her mother's intuitive sight, but brought the world of court and intrigue into their trinity. Together, they represented a formidable combination of energy and spiritual power.

They had spoken guardedly of their

belief, in the traditions of the New Learning which had swept Europe a generation previously, in education and the emancipation of women from the shackles in which the female species had for so long been confined, actually if not theoretically. Slaves of the masculine ego, domestic servants and breeders of more male children who would be taught to despise the females who bestowed the gift of life. They adhered, they told Nimue, to the superior potential, the superior wisdom of women, to the ancient power of the female as personified in the Goddess of the Old Religion.

Somewhat startled, Nimue turned interrogatively to Maire Maeve, who responded with a slight smile just touching her lips.

'The Holy Virgin, in another guise I am thinking, sister, has always been the hope of mankind,' she said in her low voice with its distinctive accent — Irish, Nimue supposed, since she was from that country. She was expressing a concept Gereint Gwynne had held himself, yet there was something else, something that underlaid her words, making them unfamiliar to Nimue's experience, something the young woman could not place.

'I studied in Rome,' Maire Maeve added pointedly, reading Nimue's unspoken thought, and once more Nimue was aware of the depths of power here. It was carefully concealed, yet in her way this woman was as formidable as the man she had begun to regard with wariness, almost certain he was her adversary, the man in the dark cloak, the Holy Devil himself.

Hospitably, she was served with sweetmeats and wine by Judith Carter's own hands, and the man who had hovered in the background — Mister Jobling, to whom the gallery, the tapestries and carved oak chests and the whole beautiful house in its gardens belonged — was presented to her.

'He too is a worshipper at the shrine of the Goddess,' Judith Carter explained, and Nimue eyed the merchant thoughtfully. The impression she had received from his presence had been of overtly masculine self-importance rather than an appreciation of the subtle power of the female. To her slight discomfiture, he came forward and leaned his stout form over her hand with an elaborately theatrical gesture that would have caused Will Shakespeare to lift his eyebrows.

'Maiden, Lady and Mistress,' he intoned, in an unexpectedly high voice that came oddly from his bulk. Unaccountably, Nimue was seized by a sudden urge to laugh, which shocked her slightly in view of the gravity of the moment, but she was sure her father and Pendragon, too, would have found this contrived pretentiousness amusing. She disengaged her fingers as soon as she could and moved away in acceptance of Judith Carter's invitation to sit beside her — this she judged to be the lesser of two evils.

'Tobias has placed his house at

our disposal,' Judith Carter confided, flashing her white teeth at Nimue. Her masses of black hair fell forward over her shoulders, and her veil was studded with tiny brilliants. There was a strong scent of patchouli about her and again Nimue was struck by her strange, hysterical energy.

In an attempt to diffuse it, the girl spoke as matter-of-factly as she could.

'Our holy sister,' she reminded them, with a slight bow in the direction of the still figure in the robe and coif, 'has indicated that I might be able to help you — or you me.' As no-one commented, she added rather more pointedly: 'I would be glad of some enlightenment.'

There was a silence, fraught with significance, then Rosalind leaned forward familiarly. Her smile was slow, amused, conspiratorial.

'I thought you had understood. Did we not speak of the Hand of Glory?'

Nimue's heart quickened.

'Then it is truly the Hand? You

know — all of you — something more of it? Something beyond the common gossip?'

The other women gathered closer. More than ever, Nimue was reminded of a group of ancient crones concentrating their attention on the working out of some spell or fate.

'The Dead Man's Hand, the Hand of Glory — that is a tale for the foolish, for those whose destiny is to live in fear of the powerful. It is the superstition of which I told you before that evening at 'the Black's,' Rosalind said with a gesture that might have signified impatience. 'Yet its influence is hypnotic, it controls sleep and so bestows power upon the mind which remains awake and alert. It may be invoked — and we invoke it — for the benefit of womankind.' She paused, then added: 'We three follow the old way. We would rid society of the childish ambitions of men. We believe that woman, not man, must rule.'

'Is this not the teaching of all of

us who hold to the ancient path? For your father told me himself that he regarded the power of the Goddess as the most potent force in the world,' Judith Carter added rather querulously, holding her little dog clutched to the gem-encrusted velvet of her bodice and stroking its fur with her long, white fingers, on which several rings glittered. Even as Nimue stared at the gems on those deliberate fingers, flashing as they caught the light, Judith pointed to the girl's own hand, from which she had removed her glove. 'You also wear her stone. It is as we thought. You are one of us.'

Nimue looked down at the heavy ring on her betrothal finger, the dim translucent depths of the moonstone that had belonged to Pendragon's mother, and something stirred painfully in her heart. There was a kind of truth here, and she must face it.

'This is indeed the stone of the Goddess, Mistress of the Night,' she murmured reluctantly. 'And my father I know reverenced her power.' She might have added that Gereint Gwynne had also reverenced other manifestations of the divine, and that she found Judith Carter's words too judgemental, too dismissive. They were clipped and brittle with impatience, and Nimue would have liked to discuss their implications rather than accept them without question, but she saw this would irritate the speaker. Instead, she was impelled to ask with difficulty:

'You say you knew him, madam? I did not know — I was not aware — .'

Judith Carter's eyes took on a rapt, unfocussed expression.

'I knew of him. And I aspired, I dared — . I approached him as I told you to offer my services as priestess, and we spoke — ah yes, he spoke to me.'

Nimue sat silently. She was puzzled and becoming increasingly uneasy. There were many things here which were familiar to her. Yet somehow, they were also foreign, but she could not put her finger on what it was that was different about them.

'You suggested I might help you,' she said again, assuming a brisk, business-like tone with a great effort, and Maire Maeve leaned forward slightly.

'You will help us, sure, if you will allow us to help you, Mistress Pendragon,' she said enigmatically.

★ ★ ★

When she emerged from the house in Chelsea, Nimue was still not quite certain of exactly what had been said. The three women, all possessed with powers to some degree, had cut across each other, answered questions that had not been asked while at the same time leaving queries that had been directly expressed, hanging like broken threads in the air.

It was obvious, she thought as she walked in the garden of her little house that evening, a cloak pulled round her against the chill from the river, that these three — witches? — knew a great deal about the Hand of Glory, though how they had come by their information was something else that had not been made clear. Did they have connections with the criminal fraternity, or had they perhaps stumbled on the Hand while pursuing their own magical affairs? No matter, that was for Robert Cecil or even Lord Burleigh to ascertain, if it proved to be relevant. She could not seriously believe that these three women — one of them a holy sister — had links with the underworld of rogues and lawbreakers, nor that they would have asked her to join them if that was the case.

They were concerned, they had told her, with the state of affairs, the status quo. Their motivation seemed clear. They believed that womankind — personified by the Goddess of ancient pagan tradition — could and should be controlling the affairs of the world.

'A Queen instead of a King, as there

has been in England?' Nimue hazarded. She did not see what relevance this obsessive feminism could have to the prospect of a threat to the peace of the country, and added rather doubtfully: 'James of Scotland will be Elizabeth's heir — you do not secretly favour some female contender for the throne, I hope?'

'Dear Madam Pendragon,' purred Maire Maeve, with a slight movement of her elegant hand, 'we have no interest in thrones nor whoever might sit upon them. Our world is of the spirit.'

At this uncompromising statement, three pairs of eyes regarded her expectantly, and Nimue found herself recalling her conviction that the image of the Hand of Glory must be a mental concept, something that threatened the soul, not the body. She nodded slowly.

'Then your wish is to safeguard the world of the spirit.'

'Adherence to the Goddess, to

Ashtoreth, to Isis, only can do it,' breathed Judith Carter. 'Oh, let us count you one of our company, one of us. For we need the strongest, the purest powers on our side.'

'On your side?' Nimue's mind seemed to be fogged, each thought an effort. 'But what then — ? But who — ?'

She opened her lips to frame the question — one that she supposed slowly, had been inevitable — but she knew the answer even before she asked it. This too, had been as inevitable as the struggle she sensed was about to come. She changed the words she had been going to utter, and spoke with certainty.

'It is true, he is the one, that 'Counsellor' — the Holy Devil. I knew it must be so. It is he, then, he who is the danger, he who is the enemy.'

They looked at each other, the silence drawn out thinly between them. Nimue wondered for a moment whether she had been mistaken, for she thought at first they had not understood her meaning. But then Maire Maeve, with a gesture of acknowledgement, said in a low, conspiratorial voice:

'Are not all men, with their arrogance, their intemperate wallowing in the troughs of the flesh, an enemy to the cool reasoning, the elevated mind of woman?'

Nimue shivered. There had been heat, passion that seared scornfully within those words — and what personal prejudice, she wondered with interest, had prompted them, strange in the mouth of a holy sister whose religion preached tolerance? — but she was aware of a sudden coolness in the atmosphere. Evil took on form when it was spoken of.

'You want me, then, to join with you to defeat this man?' she asked. 'Spiritually, I mean, for I have no temporal power.'

Again the three women looked at each other.

'You do not need to be modest with

us, sister,' Judith Carter said, with a glittering look, and Maire Maeve added softly:

'You have more ability, perhaps, than you know.'

But though these remarks were, she supposed, intended to encourage her, they had effect instead of rousing her impatience, and Nimue might have replied sharply. The truth was neither modest nor immodest, and she had never tried to measure the gifts that God had bestowed on her. Something in the accents of the woman's voice distracted her, however, stirring up renewed echoes in her mind — . For a moment, the gallery was blotted out. She was there again upon the cliffs, with the seabirds screaming — and the ship clinging like a ghost to the surface of the sea — .

Was it a waking dream? A vision? She only knew she was suspended between breaths, standing with her cloak pulled tight about her against the wind — but aware too, knowing the danger and what it portended and where it originated, so that she seemed to cry out a warning, though her voice was seized by the gale — and then it was the wine-cup Judith Carter had filled, not the folds of her cloak, that was tight in her fingers, and the carved stool on which she sat that supported her suddenly shaking body.

'*Santa Catalina*,' she moaned, with no awareness of what she was saying, and Maire Maeve retreated a step from the smoky golden blaze that burned for an instant in her eyes. The other woman, watching her, paled beneath her coif so that the bones of her face stood out starkly. She lifted her hand and crossed herself, but Nimue did not see the movement. She was speaking again in a clear voice that rang through the gallery, involuntarily yet from the depths of knowledge she could not dispute, a certainty of truth.

'It is from Ireland, from Ireland that the danger comes.' And then, in the realisation of what she had said, she caught her breath on a little sob. 'Oh, God, I was right to think so, it is as I thought — .'

As Marie Maeve articulated something that she did not grasp, the girl turned to her, trying to recover herself, struggling to compose her senses. The shifting images, the words, swam through her brain like fish in water.

'It must be him — the Holy Devil — for there is a dark angel — and the danger, the threat of the Hand, it falls from the shadow that was cast on the wild waves beyond the shores of Ireland — . You knew, you knew it all — .'

Her heart was slowing its thick, fast jerks against the bodice of her gown now, and she was able to think a little more clearly. For the moment she was only half aware of the presence of the others. She groped for words.

'If it is from Ireland, then it must be Madam O'Malley — the Irishwoman, the Irish Queen — she is against us also. A conspiracy — . Against the state — . Oh, this is treason — treason — .'

She became aware that they were watching her, their faces reflecting their reactions, frozen. Mister Jobling was staring, his eyes and his mouth open, quivering. Judith Carter seemed transfixed, in some kind of ecstacy, but Rosalind looked frightened, her youth very evident suddenly. Maire Maeve's expression she could not see. The woman's head was bent over the sinuous fingers that counted her rosary beads.

In the silence that vibrated shrilly through the gallery, the arresting of the women into stiff, unnatural poses — and her own tension — Nimue was suddenly conscious of a sense of anti-climax. Half apologetically, she shrugged.

'I did not think so of the Irish Queen, I could not believe her treacherous,' she said in a more normal tone. She felt very tired, and her head was aching.

'Nevertheless, your powers have shown

you the way,' said Rosalind, her fear dissolving into breathless excitement.

'We can count you with us, lady?' Judith Carter asked, extending her hand, and with the feeling that she had no other choice, Nimue would have nodded, but that her head seemed unaccountably heavy and stiff on her neck. Even as she moved, rousing herself to speak some sort of answer, there was a distraction. The little dog stirred and leaped from its mistress's arms, running yapping to the window in alarm. A shadow — of some large bird, perhaps — was moving there, shaking the sunlight and throwing it into bars of light and dark across the floor.

★ ★ ★

As though the current beneath the surface of a river had suddenly changed its direction, the atmosphere in the gallery became subtly transformed. Judith Carter once again swept her little dog up into her arms, where it crouched, shivering, so that her attention turned from Nimue. Rosalind went to the casement and looked out, but only the branches of the rose that would bloom when summer came, moved delicately, and she too bent over the little dog, fondling it and teasing it for following shadows.

Melisand Tournier, she told them, possessed a lapdog that would chase butterflies for hours together, and catch them in its mouth, then let them go free and never harm them. Judith smiled, and Maire Maeve, leaning towards the plump figure of Mister Jobling, enquired whether it was true that there were strange beasts such as she had heard of that carried their young in pockets made from their own fur.

The merchant replied that he did not know, but he had it on good authority from those who had travelled into lands and seas yet uncharted, that there were beasts as large as houses, with a tail at each end, and others that stored water in humps upon their backs and could live for months in sandy deserts where rain never fell. He himself, naturally, was interested in such things since his trade was in the buying and selling of pelts and skins — he had recently, he informed them, negotiated the purchase of the most beautiful white sables which were to be presented as a gift to Her Majesty — he was certain she possessed nothing to rival them — .

Lightly, the chatter rose and fell, as they spoke of irrelevancies. Who had presented what to whom, and the worth of Lady Goosens' new shoes with their gold buckles, in angels. Judith Carter and Rosalind vied with each other to enthuse over the latest colours the dyers had achieved for proposed new gowns, the way to fold the lace of a collar or a ruff, the choice of a jewel. Maire Maeve deftly introduced the subject of music — she had heard some new and merry madrigals by a composer who was generally thought to be concerned only with holy works — Byrde, she thought was his name — and, turning to the silent Nimue, she enquired did Mistress Pendragon sing, and did she like to dance? And, Rosalind asked laughing, had she dared to attempt the wicked *volta* that Her Majesty so loved?

They might have been the silliest, most empty-headed of women, finding frivolity over their sweetmeats, feeding them to Judith's little dog, tinkling laughter as they would tinkle a chime of bells. And Mister Jobling, as host, portentous in his fine clothes like some lumbering black insect that would fancy itself a dragonfly, smiled and bowed with heavy-handed gallantry as he conducted the group into the garden. They dawdled along the walk, and he presented them with what nosegays he could find among the spring flowers.

Nimue walked a little apart, glad to feel the sun on her face, the breeze ruffling her curls. She was bemused, distracted. Had it really happened, that highly charged exchange of words in the gallery, the vision of danger, swirling in mist over a grey sea? And had there really been a ship — ? What ship? What did it mean?

But even more disturbing for one who had known glimpse of other worlds since she was a child, and lived cheek-by-jowl with magic, was the uncertainty that was beginning to beset her. Could it be true that her intuitive powers had been so mistaken? Had her vision become flawed? Something was certainly very wrong, but surely not within herself, in the vision that was granted her from the light?

Her father had always warned against complacency — but had she become complacent? Had she, in accepting the Queen's directive to seek and confront the Hand of Glory, simply taken it for granted that she could not fail? The spiritual path was one of constant progression, and the most unlikely teachers could provide wisdom and instruction. She had been too facile in her judgements, she reproached herself, too quick to dismiss the three women who had confronted her in the gallery, as materialistic and lacking in genuine spirituality. Yet they had spoken of offering help to her, as well as requesting it for themselves. Was this in fact the more subtle gift they could give her, a lesson in humility rather than a request for her to join them in power?

Torn by increasing doubt, she responded stiffly to their conversation as best she might for politeness' sake, taking some comfort from the familiarity of the herb scents that rose from the parterres. They brought Pendragon's wild garden and her own modest plot beside the Thames, vividly close. She recovered her self-possession enough to make a few direct enquiries as to the action the three women proposed to take against the Holy Devil, in view of the fact that they seemed to be in possession of something as terrible as a treasonable plot. Surely, she suggested, it would be better to pass on the information to the proper authorities, they could not mean to keep the knowledge to themselves.

'When the moment is right, all will be done that needs to be done,' Maire Maeve assured her calmly, and Judith Carter breathed, into the fur of her little dog:

'When she is needed, the Goddess is always ready.'

'We will speak again,' Maire Maeve told Nimue significantly, as she climbed at last into Mister Jobling's coach to be driven home. 'With words and with intent, as sisters.'

'When it is time,' added Judith Carter, and Rosalind flashed her one of her most glittering glances, and laid a finger across her own lips.

★ ★ ★

Intrigue, hearsay, the clinging cobwebs of conspiracy. They had blurred and blotted out the sharpness of her mind. But when she tried to clarify her impressions once she was alone, she decided that the most significant thing she had discovered was that the threat of the Hand of Glory was no subtle one, no image denoting spiritual arrogance to damn the spirit. It had proved to be, predictably, far more prosaic, the manifestation of human greed, weakness, manipulation and ambition.

Glad of the freshness of the evening air, needing it around her to revive and cleanse her of the invasive, suffocating atmosphere of the afternoon, she supposed that in fairness to the three women, she should be grateful in spite of the fact that her meeting with them had tired her and left her in low spirits. They meant well, and perhaps had wittingly or unwittingly taught her a valuable spiritual lesson. Surely this was cause for thankfulness.

Yet she found she could summon up only a weary distaste for the whole business. The task she had been assigned had turned itself in the end into a petty, sordid affair, something far removed from the fearsome confrontation she had anticipated, where she had might have risked her soul.

Her father had often told her that evil was petty, that it was a little thing, which must dress itself in borrowed authority to sway the credulous. She had seen that in Gilbert Stoneyathe, who had looked at her across the width of his chamber at Grannah, guilt furtive in his eyes as the cry went up from the courtyard of Ralph Tollaster's murder. Her father had been right, she saw now, resting her head against the worn stone of the gate that led to the water-steps and gazing at the softly gathering evening light on the river.

Her husband too had possessed the wisdom to see and speak the truth when he had called Gilbert a petty tyrant. For all that he had murdered, for all that he had the ability to cause suffering, Gilbert Stoneyathe was a little, little man.

And now, involved in the secret machinations that attempted to dignify themselves with the title of Hand of Glory, it seemed that here was another. In the quiet of the garden with the light dim and tinged with streaks of orange, the last of the sunset giving way to shadows of deep violet, Nimue faced her feelings towards this man she hardly knew as honestly as she could.

It was here that the true source of her disillusion lay, not in the loud and divergent personalities of the women, she was forced to admit. For whatever he was, the fleeting occasions when she had encountered him had marked her awareness of him in letters of fire that would be difficult to obliterate. He was someone, Nimue had been convinced, whose power was not of the ordinary, who might if he had so desired, have set his seal on designs of cosmic magnitude. Was it possible that he was none of these, that he was after all nothing more than another little man, demeaned by his greed for temporal power and the things of this world? And if it was so, why did the thought disturb her?

It was obvious, even though the three women had not actually said so, that this enemy of the people, the so-called Counsellor, the Holy Devil, was no magus. He was nothing greater than a politically-motivated agitator, in league (she shrugged the prospect angrily away) with the militant Irish. Exploiting — or being exploited by — the Irishwoman who bore a name that in her own land was more ancient than that of Elizabeth Tudor.

Yet another who aspired to personal power but cloaked it with the catch-phrases that always justified such men's activities. What would his particular cause be, Nimue found herself wondering scornfully. 'Freedom'? 'Democracy'? 'Religious tolerance'?

In her attempts to be honest with herself, she was acutely discomfited to find that she was actually disappointed — and angry — because a man she had begun to consider some great magus of the dark, whose stature might have rivalled Doctor Dee, or the sinister Simon Forman who she knew was claimed to consort with devils to gain his own ends — or even, if he had chosen the left-hand path instead of the light, her own father — was in reality nothing but a pawn to politics, tangled in a web of activities that might destroy men's lives, but could not touch the soul. And she had been preparing herself for a confrontation with true spiritual power, however misguided, something that might threaten the deepest values of human living, wielded by an adversary she could at least respect.

She felt her lips curl into a rueful little smile as, almost, she seemed to hear her father's voice, half-encouraging, half-chiding.

'So you would have fought a great battle against the dark, child, and now weep that your enemy is not worth your sword? Remember humility, shine only for the sake of shining. You do not know which are the true battles nor whether they are won or lost, Nimue. Leave that to God.'

Tears stung her eyes, but she did not know whether they were of anger or sorrow. Perhaps it was not intended that she should be the instrument to defy the Hand of Glory. Perhaps she had been too proud, even, of her name as a Pendragon. She bit her lip. She was suddenly cold, and aware that she was hungry as well as tired. Huw would be serving her supper, but before she went in, she stood for a moment with bent head while she placed herself and the events of the day before the higher power that dwelt beyond the silver moon she could see rising beyond the trees on the other side of the river, beyond the sunset and the dawn.

The recollection came into her mind of the painted card where the star had burned steadily. And also of the card with the dangerous, galloping horses that lurched the chariot. She was unaccountably comforted at the thought that final decisions were not in her hands. She need only hold fast to the light, no more than that would be expected or exacted from her.

8

But in the morning, Nimue awoke with a sense of weariness, and in spite of the sunlight, her mood was sombre. She recognised her sense of depletion as the aftermath of her encounter with individuals who had each exuded power and, she thought dispassionately, were prepared to use it to gain their own ends — whether those ends were justified or not.

She had encountered this same phenomenon in the past, though never before alone, without the strengthening presence of her father. He had explained to her that there were some people, often highly gifted with spiritual awareness, who had a debilitating rather than an uplifting effect on others because in spite of all their apparent learning, they had nevertheless not progressed far enough along the road to true wisdom to recognise that real power came from complete submission of their own will to that of God — in whatever form they might perceive him.

Such people, Gereint Gwynne had told his daughter with a frown darkening his eyes, were unable to achieve their true potential since their own wishes, their own solutions to the problems that beset the world, were more important to them than their place in any greater pattern, though the web of Wyrd is woven through time and space and takes no account of the spark, for it burns with the complete flame.

'Good people they may be, some of them, in the eyes of the world — saints even,' Gereint had said. 'And often by the sheer force of their will, they are the ones who achieve feats that seem to be miracles. Hailed as saviours, even, such things have been known. And yet — if that was the way of it, if the will was all, why did Our Lord accept the cross and not choose to march with an army to claim his kingdom? We cannot know

God's will, child, none of us, and it is the greatest sin of all to presume to teach him his business.'

Now, as she gazed from her casement unseeing at the waking garden while she put on her cap before she went down to begin the work of the day, Nimue wondered about those three women. Maire Maeve, for instance. Whose curiously unrevealing eyes reflected only what was around her, and for some reason this morning, reminded the girl of the eyes of a snake or a lizard. Cold eyes, yet how they had seemed to smoulder with purpose. One could not, surely, imagine that someone so disciplined, so filled with apparent holiness, was anything but good. And yet — considering the matter, Nimue found it impossible to picture that finely-drawn, ascetic face crumpled in humility before the altar, the sculptured lips ever bringing themselves to murmur: 'Thy will be done.'

It was true, she thought. Whatever

great work Maire Maeve envisaged, whether as a crusade against the threat of the Hand or not, there was pride in her, and more than pride. The curse that could so easily fall upon any great intellect — that of spiritual arrogance.

Turning her heavy moonstone on her finger, Nimue began to wonder anew about the details which had so far not been revealed to her. What plan, for instance, did the Holy Devil — possessor of an awesomely powerful mind whose measure she had already, most disturbingly, taken — have in view, what scheme which threatened the peace of England? To depose the Queen and seize the throne himself — to assist some foreign power in overthrowing the government? Somehow Nimue could not believe it. The man was above all, no fool, and she was certain that if he involved himself in any plot it would be far more subtle than that.

But whatever it was, it was presumably known to the three women (the three witches, as she would always regard them in spite of herself), and they had some sort of proposal in mind to oppose him. But though they had sought her out to join them, they had not seemingly approached any of the Queen's ministers, the appointed representatives of the people. Or did they have supporters in the government, whom they had not mentioned to her? She recollected that Robert Cecil knew nothing of them beyond reputation — which he had not been inclined to regard very favourably. It was altogether a prospect that Nimue found increasingly frustrating, and she could not help thinking that this in itself must hold significance, for was not all truth of such shining simplicity that it did not need explaining?

She tried again to clarify her impressions. The three — the sisterhood — had said they believed in the superiority of woman, and Nimue had sensed that even Mister Jobling, who had placed his house at their disposal, was not included in their confidence except as a kind of acolyte. The superiority of woman. Suddenly she remembered Robert Cecil's remark about Judith Carter and her dead husbands. 'Mister Jobling had best take care.' The superiority of woman — power — . However she viewed the situation it became no clearer and no less frustrating.

The unease she had felt on awaking began to increase. They were working in the name of the Goddess, Judith Carter had said. Isis? Ashtoreth? Nimue was familiar with the cult of the goddess, and like her father did not underestimate the strength of the Maiden, the Lady and the Ancient Hag. Yet even the goddess recognised the necessity for a consort, the male without whom she was not truly able to achieve her own rightful feminine strength and identity. The goddess respected the power of the male, she did not seek to destroy or diminish it, but to use it to balance her own.

Nimue tried to recall exactly what

had been said about the intentions of the three women. Had they actually spoken of working on behalf of the people, confronting some foreign threat to the Queen and the kingdom, or merely of power — power for its own sake — ?

'You do not know your own power, let us help you to become aware of it.'

'We believe that women, not men, should rule in the world.'

And yet — 'We are not concerned with thrones or those who sit upon them.'

Had she grossly mistaken their meaning, she wondered, her heart beginning to thump unevenly so that her blood pounded in her head and her vision blurred. But if they considered the Counsellor — the Holy Devil — an enemy, and they had sought to persuade her to join her powers to theirs — ('we need the strongest, the purest on our side', Judith Carter had said), then what else could they intend but to oppose him and the Hand of Glory?

Nimue's mind was unravelling thoughts as though they spun from a spool. A tale for the credulous, Rosalind Blackcross had said of the Hand — and yet it has the power of controlling sleep — and thus of bestowing power on the mind that remains awake and alert — . Nimue wondered with a sharp concentration, exactly what the power that came from controlling sleep might have to do with confronting the Counsellor — . And what relevance it had to his own intentions towards England — whatever they might be — .

The complexities of the matter required some thought, particularly in view of her own feelings of spiritual depletion after only a few hours in the company of the women. For as her father had many times reminded her, the body may become weary from any effort, physical or mental, but the spirit is never lessened only as a result of dark or negative influence.

Trying to see her way through the

mists, concentrating yet aware too of the sounds of the city stirring, the street cries and call of the watermen already at work in their boats, black against the shining water of the Thames, Nimue seemed to feel the great heart of London beating all around her, the pulse of the city over which, she was sure, Elizabeth the Queen brooded on mornings when she too found it difficult to sleep and wrestled with demons who would have threatened her kingdom, her people, the trust that had been placed upon her together with her crown.

It was an awesome burden, as was any responsibility for others, and one where more than ever the wise man had to be aware of the delicate balance that was needed between the many conflicting pressures and interests so that the will of providence could work in whatever way it must, yet tempered by human endeavour towards the greatest good of all. And Elizabeth's concern must of necessity range far beyond the shores of her kingdom, to where the threat to peace might come. Ireland, for instance, had been a simmering pot to the crown of England from time immemorial — . A back door to invasion, Robert Cecil had said, in spite of the fact that there were many Irish who were men of great honour and integrity — statesmen whose word was inviolate, who could be trusted — .

Even the Irish Queen, Grainne O'Malley, was a very great lady. Nimue found herself recollecting the impression the woman had made upon her at 'the Black's'. She had been so certain that Madam O'Malley would not stoop to dishonour, how could she have been mistaken? And why did a sense of increasing unease tighten the muscles of her body and lift the hairs on the back of her neck as though in warning when she thought about Ireland?

The back door to invasion — . She was remembering fragments of intuitive awareness suddenly, of the words she had spoken to Robert Cecil at the apothocary's shop — about the Spanish fleet, the great and terrifying Armada which had been driven by the winds and weather (and perhaps also by the endeavours of those who, like her father and Pendragon and those gifted with the power, had worked secretly across the length and breadth of England) — to an awful doom on the rocks of the Scottish coasts and off Ireland — .

Unmoving, still at the window of her chamber but unaware of her surroundings, Nimue bit her lip thoughtfully. Ireland again — invasion — . Yet Robert Cecil had dismissed the prospect of Spanish invasion, though there had been many times when the street-corner orators and sheet-mongerers drove rumour wildly from place to place and the citizens of London ran to huddle in their homes in fear that there would soon be booted Spanish troops in their cuirasses and striped gold and red tramping through the streets of the city.

Spanish invasion had been a spectre that had haunted public consciousness throughout Elizabeth's reign, and the King of Spain was a familiar figure held up as a never-failing deterrent to naughty children, like the devil only worse.

The back door to invasion — the phrase insinuated itself yet again into Nimue's mind. It might not be the Irish people themselves who were the threat, for if Grainne O'Malley was openly at the court and on familiar terms with Elizabeth — bidden to supper as an honoured guest at 'the Black's' — was it likely that the Queen and her advisers would be unaware of possible treachery — ?

No, others who were nameless and formless might seek to enter by the back door of Ireland — . The threat might be suspected, yet only on the periphery of men's vision, hidden and dank as a cloud that carried a deadly pestilence, yet insinuating as fog, something that brought some undefinable alarm to men's eyes and was spoken of in whispers, guardedly and in fear, as the wrath of God — . Or the Hand of Glory — .

Nimue was breathing fast, her eyes turned inwards. She was no longer within the confines of her chamber but stood again — though she was not aware of how she came there — on the great cliffs of Moher at the end of the world. She was shivering with the wild light and air and the foam from spray that drenched her in its silver and sable mist, like a breath that hung over the sea, blurring it against the sky. Her inner eye saw once more the ship, as it clung to the surface of the waves, and the black dot that was a boat, making its way to the shore. There was a cloak about her shoulders, and long tangled tresses of hair whipped out round her head. Her hands gripped themselves together, and she could feel the hardness of bone beneath the flesh.

Did she live some other life on that

far shore, then, or was it her own soul that had journeyed across time and place to give her a message, a glimpse, a warning against — .

And again she found her lips forming the words she had spoken in the gallery of Mister Jobling's house.

'*Santa Catalina.*'

Maire Maeve had said she was calling on the saints, but Nimue realised with a quickening of her heart that she had spoken involuntarily, and that the words must mean something. She had known, in her vision, that there was danger, and she had been aware of what it was, and where to look for it and find it — . Again she was on the cliffs, straining her eyes to look out to where the ship lay. It was too far to read the name that was painted on the galleon's prow, beneath the scrolled carving of gilt and ebony, elaborately upholding the figure of a woman with long flowing hair and lifted hands, eyes turned to heaven — the saint whose protection lay over the vessel, who interceded for the sailors in the face of storm and tempest — the saint who was called — .

Nimue's breath caught in her throat. Her eyes, unseeing, gazed even deeper inward.

'*Santa — Santa Catalina.*'

★ ★ ★

When she went down she summoned Math and instructed him to go to the apothecary's in the Strand. She quickly penned a letter requesting a meeting with Mister Cecil as soon as it could be arranged, for whatever his private opinion of the Lady Ardua and the Holy Devil, and however little credence he might place on Judith Carter's claims to supernatural power, he must be told of what she had heard and what she suspected. When she had placed the matter in his hands it would be for him — or his father or some other servant of the crown — to take whatever action they considered appropriate. Once again she reminded herself that it was not for her to take such momentous decisions. Her part was to identify the evil and only assume what responsibility she could as a confronter of such threats as lay beyond the scope of the temporal — or the authorised teachings of the church.

With a slight easing of her disquiet now that some action was being taken, she watched Math ride away, and then turned back to the house, resolving to blow the webs of suspicion and intrigue from her mind with physical labour and apply herself to the removal of honest to goodness dirt and grime instead of dark fogs that obscured the mind. Kilting up her skirts and wrapping herself in an apron of coarse sacking, she seized pail and twigs and set herself to cleaning the stone flags of the dairy and pantry and the little chamber she used as a stillroom.

She was sitting back on her heels, regarding the whitened floor of the dairy with satisfaction when Huw came smiling, soft-footed in his white robes, to summon her to the hall, where a familiar figure waited, lounging easily against the black oak chest. Nimue's spirits lifted at the sight of him. She felt his appearance could not have been more opportune.

'Will,' she cried, and impulsively she threw off her housewife's apron, touched her unruly hair into a semblance of order beneath her cap, and swept him into the parlour, where she seated herself lightheartedly and bade him do the same, calling for Tib, the little maid who with her sister Tab, had somehow (at Mistress Grabbon's instigation) become attached to the household.

These two, like small scuttling rabbits, were to be encountered earnestly mopping or polishing in dim corners of the rooms and stairs, or passing with arms filled with spotlessly clean linen. They tossed the feather beds and pummelled pillows and bolsters with a diligence instilled by their youth (for they were scarcely more than children), and their reverence, tinged with fearful worship, for their employer, Madam Pendragon. In spite of her kindness and beauty, they had been terrified of her at first — or rather, of her reputation — for had not her father been the most sinister of wizards who could work all sorts of magic and spells? They had sweated nervously in case they might not give satisfaction for who knew, the daughter of a wizard, if displeased, could probably do far worse than beat her servants, and might transform them into toads or bats.

However, the sight of Nimue bustling about the house just like any other goodwife concerned with the business of parlour and kitchen, singing as she spared Mistress Grabbon's joints by getting on her knees to do her own scrubbing, or with her arms deep in the suds on washing day and her pretty hair smudged beneath her cap — all these had begun to reassure them. And they had discovered that there were worse terrors than those represented by their young mistress.

It was Madam Pendragon who had dispelled their panic when they had first encountered Huw with his dark skin and strangely white hair and eyes. Through chattering teeth, the girls had sobbed out their conviction that they had fallen into the clutches of a devil who would surely kill them and eat them, and it had been Nimue who had had to coax them from the depths of the dog-kennel to which they had fled to crouch together in the hope that Bran the mastiff would protect them against Huw's supposed black arts.

* * *

Will had his lute slung across his shoulder, and he struck a few plaintive chords and sang a verse or two with a languishing air and a doleful sighing in Nimue's direction before he tasted the ale that little Tib respectfully placed before him.

'Oh, no lovesickness or tragedy, Will,' the girl pleaded, laughing. 'Let us have something merry. It is not like you to be sad, and I — . Well, this morning I have a desire to be feckless and foolish. Have you nothing else, a round or a dance?'

He gave her a quizzical glance and then tapped his foot. Another melody rippled from the strings in counterpoint to his voice.

'Under the greenwood tree,
Who loves to lie with me
And tune his merry note
Unto the sweet bird's throat — .
With a hey and a ho
And a hey nonny no.
Sweet lovers love the spring.'

Nimue's eyes were bright, green-gold as the morning sun that was warming on the leaves outside the casement. She looked as youthful as little Tib, and had pushed all thoughts of the Hand, plots and treason and conspiracies, out of her head. It was a wonderful gift, but one which all might enjoy if they chose to do it, her father had often said, the ability to live only in the moment and to savour each moment to the full. Nimue's heart lifted in sudden thankfulness for the joys she was blessed with — a spring morning, sunlight and a dear friend beside her. Pastime and good company, as the Queen's father, King Henry, had written. What more could the heart desire?

It was not irresponsible to leave off caring and being concerned sometimes, Gereint Gwynne had said. To dwell on nothing but the abundance in living had a habit of putting everything into its proper perspective, and problems which had seemed insurmountable would mysteriously disappear. A sense of gladness and thankfulness for gifts bestowed had the power to wipe out in some mysterious fashion, the need for all else, including answers.

So Nimue laughed at Will, clapped her hands like a child and joined in the round as she sat with her kilted skirts and tousled dark curls. She knew a great easing of her troubled spirits. In the end, somehow, all would be well, and for the moment Will had brought her an unexpected reprieve from duty and responsibility — . And from other undercurrents she was afraid to consider, for their significance was too disturbing. Whatever plots were afoot, whoever was behind the threat of the Hand, she found herself personally frightened — and angry because she was frightened — by the power of the man in the dark cloak. The Holy Devil.

Oh, she had been aware before that he had power, but inexplicably, he seemed much more powerful now that she suspected he was no magus, simply another political agitator. She had been convinced before that he was not what he seemed and could not be trusted. But now she knew what he really was, and why he was a threat, she found her uneasiness had not been alleviated but was increasing (in a dark corner at the back of her mind) almost to a kind of panic. For if he was no magus, and had no power that she recognised, how could he disturb her peace to the extent he had done so?

Somewhat confusedly, she had begun to feel that no-one — particularly no *man* was to be trusted. Even Will — her dear friend Will, whose presence now, sitting here beside her, was an anchor that kept her steady in the midst of all kinds of emotional whirlpools, Will who was a link with her father and all that was sane and wise in her life — even Will was not what he seemed, not what he would appear to be. For was he not a married man with a wife and children living to whom he owed loyalty, not some young *braggadocio* gallant — .

She became aware suddenly that he was leaning forward, peering into her eyes.

'Nimue! What ails you, girl? You have a look so fey and wild I would think you had seen the devil himself.'

She could not answer, but suddenly her father's voice was warning, counselling in her ears.

'There is no dark magic, Nimue, but what we accept ourselves, no dark power save what credence we ourselves give to evil. And the greatest weapon the dark can wield is to persuade us to doubt the light.'

For a moment, enlightenment swept in a wide swathe through her mind. Was it possible that her fears, her doubts even of Will, whom she trusted and knew to be the most honourable of men — for all that he was also a human being, with a human being's weaknesses and prey to temptations — was it possible that all the negative emotions which were, and had been besetting her were not of her own volition, but had been sent from the source of the true threat not just to the country and to men's bodies but to their souls also, as she had suspected? Even as the idea came to her, she felt a surge of power and knew she was right. The Hand of Glory — or whatever was the threat to England and Elizabeth — was no mere political thing. It was indeed something far more subtle.

But that meant —

She could not for the moment consider exactly what it did mean, save that she was suddenly, unerringly sure that her early judgements, her inner vision, had not been flawed. She should have listened to her father's whispered counsel when she had looked at the cards and viewed the galloping horses and the lurching chariot that carried her forward to an unknown destiny.

'Have faith in yourself,' he had murmured, the echo of his voice as reassuring as a quiet hand laid on her shoulder.

Nimue caught her breath as words heard long since and forgotten, came back to her also.

'It is a foolish man who never doubts,

but the wise man accepts doubts for what they are — steps to the truth. And to doubt the truth is to set ourselves before God and thus give power to the devil.'

She was seized with a great sense of release. All would indeed be well, in whatever way it must be, but she was free from this moment of the crippling doubts which had blotted out her vision of the light. It had never faded nor faltered, but had been there throughout all her doubting. She was suddenly frightened anew, but only at how nearly she had allowed herself to be duped by the enemy. But no longer. She knew him now for what he truly was. Perhaps the three women had been misled, but she was certain the threat of the Holy Devil — and the Hand of Glory — was something invasive, personal — and it was something she must prepare herself to — inevitably, when she must — fight with no assistance from Robert Cecil or his father. For they could not help her. She must do this alone.

'You need to laugh again, girl,' said Will, eying her consideringly. Her awareness had taken place within the space of a single indrawn breath. 'Leave your housewifery. I have come to take you to town, I will show you the sights if you will idle away an hour with me. And tonight — well, I have been instructed to invite you to the play. Our company is bidden to entertain at a wedding feast.'

Nimue looked up, making an effort to concentrate on his words. She felt she needed at this moment to hold onto something that was ordinary, something that was everyday.

'The play? What is the play, Will?'

'Oh, a scribbling of mine — for I have been busy lately. Scenes — . Interludes — the musicians, songs and a masque,' he told her airily, then struck a pose, wringing his hands with melodramatic fervour. 'What do you say to an excellent tragical tale of two star-crossed lovers, that will weep all your tears out of you and leave you free as air? I thought of you often, my Dark Lady, when I was penning it, and because you are there in the verse, lovely as quicksilver or a strange flower that blooms only by moonlight, I would have you watch tonight. Besides,' he added, smiling and relaxing from his tragedian's stance, 'Cuthbert Burbage is anxious that you should see some of our new work. He still has hopes you will become a benefactress of the Theatre — though he has safeguarded himself against the fickleness of woman by brewing up plans for expansion when the new season is able to open — . Do not frown so concerned, girl, I told you the Burbages will never be poor.'

Nimue felt drawn back into the familiar reality by his easy gossip, awareness that the small things of life still continued, removed from the darkly glistening threads of treason, plots and spiritual intrigue. She told herself she would think of it later, when the implications had become clearer in her mind. One could have too much of anything, even the spiritual struggle, for as Gereint Gwynne had often said, 'We cannot dwell in two worlds, and it is sufficient to live well in one. If we were meant to be saints, we would doubtless not find ourselves on this earth, but our maker — for reasons of his own and in his wisdom — has created us in the flesh.'

Will, very solid, masculine and physical, seemed to ground Nimue to the earth and give her a footing that was simple, common-sensical, drawing her back from her revelations, her wanderings into other time and place. For all his writer's vision, he was real and his reality brought her an awareness of her own.

'You are good for me, Will,' she told him, smiling, and he grinned at her, relieved to see she had lost the wild look from her face.

'Then you are a fool, girl. I am weaving the web in which I mean to ensnare you, baiting the trap, setting the primrose path before your feet. I have not given up the hope of you yet. Like Mephistopheles, I am a slavering wolf who skitters innocently in the guise of a little lambkin, to catch his dinner.'

'It is you that is the Fool,' she laughed, absurdly pleased. She found his exaggerated declarations of devotion fond and heartening now that whatever passion there had been between them was past. His acceptance of her love for Pendragon, his awareness of her grief at her husband's loss, gave her strength and courage, and the friendship that united them now was worth far more than any amount of passion or pleading. Considering everything, she thought that a day in Will's company, idling through the city and then attending the play — for all that he had promised her it was heart-wrenching and would make her weep — was exactly what she needed.

★ ★ ★

They lingered in Paul's Yard, where the booksellers were calling the merits of their wares. The arcades of the great cathedral were the haunt of all who would be a part of the bustling life of the city, from the apprentices with their street battles and their shrill calls of 'Clubs' that set honest citizens scattering, to country folk, open-mouthed in wonder, in their Sunday best, the prey of cut-purses and double-dealers. Women in scented silks, their faces painted and provoking behind masks, swept through the crowd distainfully on their high shoes, and gallants with curled and pomaded love-locks tossed back their short cloaks to reveal puffed and slashed doublets and the curve of a leg in elegant hose. Lawyers and men of business, with their clerks scurrying behind them, hurried impassively on unspecified errands, and poets proclaimed their verses, ballad-singers loudly sang and proffered their ballad sheets.

'This is the hub of the world,'

Will had said, as they wandered along companionably, watching the moving crowd. 'The glories of Venice, the splendours of Greece and Rome, Athens itself, the cradle of civilisation, what is it but London in another guise, and what the Athenians but human souls secretly struggling in their endeavours. That is perhaps the secret of it all, girl, to see that the world is different, yet it is all the same.'

Nimue turned to him, smiling. Her face was still alight with pleasure from watching the 'motions' of the puppeteers in Fleet Street. She had left all her problems uncompromisingly behind her for the day.

'You make it all so simple — wisdom — Will.'

But he was not listening. His gaze was turned to where the smoke from the city chimneys daubed the sky.

'One day,' he said, 'one day — one day — they will be selling folios here of my plays.'

Nimue wrinkled her brow, catching

the note of bravado, of hesitancy. Will was challenging fate again. He saw her look and laughed a little awkwardly, turning away.

'Come, smile girl,' he mocked her. 'Shall I not owe my fame to you and your flinty heart? For if you had not made me suffer, could I have made my audience weep — as they surely will — when young Romeo drinks poison and his Juliet stabs herself with his dagger, for the sake of love?'

Nimue's mouth curved unwillingly and she put her arm through his as they strolled on. The bells of all of London's churches swelled, pealing, tolling and jangling to announce the hour, and when the clamour had abated somewhat so that she only had to shout above the hubbub of the crowds, the street sellers, she commented with amusement:

'Whose is the wedding tonight? I fear the poor bride and her groom are doomed, since you intend to give them such a play on their wedding day, so full of poison and stabbing.

Are they so mismatched that you feel you must take the opportunity to warn them of the possible consequences of their union? Or is it that you have developed an aversion to all weddings, not just this one?'

Will made an expansive gesture.

'Oh, we will not be playing the whole tragedy,' he revealed airily. 'It is not rehearsed — hardly completed, even, for the Book.' He kissed his fingers into the air. 'The lovers will meet only, at a masked ball, and speak to each other from a balcony. As for the bride and groom, I do not know them. But Cuthbert is rubbing his hands, for their nuptuals are of some note, the family noble and, thankfully, glad to be patrons of the Theatre. Kin to the Lady Ardua, it appears. We are bid to their house in Richmond.'

Even in the brightness of the day, Nimue felt a chill as though a slight, cold wind touched her skin. She repressed a little shiver. Wherever she turned, she could not escape from intrigue, the shadow of the mad old woman with her deep eyes, and the man in the dark cloak. And behind them, formless and dim, the presence of someone — if not the Irishwoman, Grainne O'Malley, then someone nameless and faceless — reaching with bloody hands for — what?

'Oh, she has kinsfolk, then?' She made it sound careless, amused. The thought should have reassured her, she supposed. A woman, however eccentric, who had relatives who married, held wedding feasts and hired musicians and players, was a recognised member of ordered society, no midnight hag of demonic conjuring who consorted with practitioners inclined towards the powers of darkness.

Will grinned.

'An ancient name, as I thought. All families, however noble, have some such dependent, someone they might prefer not to acknowledge. And though Cuthbert sends his compliments and requests your attendance at the play, it was Ardua who remarked to me that you were pale-cheeked and pining, and bade me invite you to accompany us to the feast.'

'Indeed,' Nimue said slowly, and after a moment, Will turned to look at her.

'What is it, girl? There is a shadow walks with you and casts its dark web to catch your feet.' He hesitated, then asked in a low voice: 'Is it well with you, Nimue? The gossip you wormed from me, I have heard nothing more definite of it, the Hand of Glory. And I thought you well protected by the authorities, and your Afric angel with his eyes of pale fire and your squire who carries, unknowing, the airy shield of virtue and the sword given to those only who are chosen to wield it. No harm can come to you while they are with you. Yet the dregs of the city have a far reach, have they somehow been able to touch your heart and your peace?'

His eyes were stern, close and

concerned for her. But she shook her head. For all Will's intuitive artistic vision, for all his street wisdom, she did not think he could help her further. He had told her all he knew, and there were some burdens, her father had taught her, that could not and should not be shared.

'I think,' she said slowly, 'I think perhaps I was recalling another wedding — and another wedding feast.'

9

The carts of the players, laden with the tinsel trappings of their trade, the velvets and fustians, the Venetian masks and face paints, the elaborate curled wigs twined with ribbons and feathers, had reached their destination and now stood silent in the dark, emptied of their finery. Within the hall of the Richmond house of Lady Ardua's kinsfolk, the actors had transformed themselves into Veronese nobility, celebrating a magnificent masked ball. Benjamin Ashe, splendid as an imposing Lord Capulet, nodded gracious approval while his 'daughter', sloe-eyed Juliet, passed from partner to partner, treading the measures of the dance.

Ardent young Romeo, heir to the Montagues, had eyes for no other, and eloquently eulogised his love from where he was lurking behind a pillar.

'Oh, she doth teach the torches to
    burn bright,
It seems she hangs upon the cheek
    of night
Like to a rich jewel in an Ethiop's
    ear.'

Will had told Nimue that he regarded
this evening's performance of scenes
from his new play as in the nature
of a rehearsal, which would help him
to see how the structure shaped up on
the stage. He was in the improvised
tiring-house now with the 'Book' in
his hands, considering the effects of his
words and verses with a dispassionate,
professional eye. Meanwhile, to the
accompaniment of the musicians, the
players moved through the formalised
steps of the galliard and the carole.
Nimue, together with all the other
guests at the wedding feast, watched
lost in the magic as the sinuous figures
of doomed Romeo and Juliet, in Italian
gown and doublet, posed and mouthed
the words Will had put on their lips.

In the main body of the hall, the real bride and groom, flower-crowned and vibrant with love, had eyes only for each other. Nimue had smiled as she saw them drink from the loving cup, and then rise to lead the dancing, encouraged by shouts and joviality from their kinsfolk. The bride's hair flowed in waves of flax fairness to her waist, and was elaborately plaited and woven with ribbons. Her gown was of russet and green.

To the sound of the viol and the sackbut, figures weaved in and out, many masked and Nimue stood alone watching the scene, letting the music and the merriment play around her. She tried to respond to it, but in spite of herself, she could not. Her heart was drawn back to that other wedding and that other feast — sops in milk, and wine beside the fire in the hermit's cell — .

A long thin shape materialised beside her, the purple mask unable to disguise the fact that this apparition was the

Lady Ardua. She was unexpectedly garbed in a black Spanish farthingale in the style of the previous generation, which softened the lines of her angular figure with its silken folds, and a black lace mantilla, dripping with dark jewels of jet and black crystal sat crookedly upon her crop of brindled hair.

'Mistress Pendragon. You are welcome,' she pronounced, adding reprovingly: 'Though I see you are using the present occasion as an excuse to indulge in fruitless nostalgia. Concerning your own nuptuals, no doubt.'

Nimue's breath went out in a gasp, both at her accusatory tone and at the accuracy of the words. She looked up and saw that the eyes behind the purple mask were deeper and more piercing than she remembered, filled with shifting depths of secrets. Something like fear gripped her. There was a power at work here that she did not understand.

'Why — should you believe so?' she managed to ask, in a low voice, and

Lady Ardua stared at her consideringly.

'You are very young to be a widow,' she said at length. 'Too young. I have said before, Mistress Pendragon, you need a husband, one who will supervise your thinking and put an end to such melancholy fancies.'

Her words seemed to pierce Nimue to the soul, and the anger that seethed as though from a physical wound, prompted the girl to speech before she could think, before she could remember the wisdom of her father, or her own dignity.

'And how, madam, do you propose I should defy the fate that took my husband from me? Use necromancy to raise my lord's dear form from the grave?'

The music and laughter of the wedding feast seemed to have faded into a dim meaningless hum that was very far away. Only her own words spat bitingly into Lady Ardua's face, and the fast beat of her heart thrumming with the movement of her pulse, the tiny indrawn panic of her breath, were loud in the sudden intensity of the moment. For what seemed eternities, as time stood still, she gazed into the dark blue of the eyes begind the mask. Then Ardua said mildly:

'Really, such extremes are quite uncalled for, child. I can only attribute this lack of judgment to your newly widowed state. Naturally, the answer is that you will have to take another husband — and the sooner the better, in my opinion. Otherwise, who knows where your uncertain temperament may lead you.'

'Another husband?' Nimue could hardly believe her ears, and the sounds from the company seemed to rush from their far distance towards her, now thrumming very loudly in her head. Fury possessed her, but Lady Ardua ignored the blaze of green-gold that would have shrivelled her to nothing. She turned away briskly, as though she had wasted enough time.

'There are plenty of men — even

here — for you to choose from, child,' she said bracingly, and added in such a different tone that Nimue thought she must have imagined the words: 'Choose wisely.'

She had gone into the laughing throng. A man in the crimson satin of a Blackamoor, with a dark mask covering his face, loomed before Nimue, holding out his hand, but she gave a little cry and shrank from him. All her senses were in a turmoil, anger and grief, passion and pain, lifting her out of herself, as though she was spinning helplessly, lost and unable to grasp at anything to save herself.

The image of the speeding horses pulling the chariot on — on — came to her mind. She looked round desperately for Will, but found herself instead swept up by the dancers. The young bridegroom was laughing on her right hand, his dark eyes mocking her and the bride, fresh and sweet as the morning, had seized her left wrist in slim fingers. To the rhythm of the drum, the melody of the pipes and the viols, Nimue gave herself up to whatever would take her, swept uncaring, unaware into the steps of the dance.

She let go of all attempts to control her anguish and despair, her fury at her own impotence, her inability to change the world, fate, destiny, or bring back her husband from the grave. She was swung from one partner to the next, helpless as a doll, a puppet, and she found she was crying and yet laughing through her tears, while all the time the pulse of the music beat relentlessly through her, on and on and on.

★ ★ ★

And somewhere in that mad hour, at some moment she could not identify, she became intoxicatingly aware with a sensation of disbelief, yet an intense, predestined acceptance of something beyond the scope of reality, that a miracle had happened.

She had felt it around her, power,

great power, but the true force of it stunned her. And if it was nothing but an illusion, brought into being by magic, then was the magic black or white? For (she tried to tell herself, as she sought to keep some kind of a hold on reality) it might not be in the interests of the higher powers that she should be lifted from despair to delirious happiness, from such depths of grief to the pinnacles of joy. Even the intensity of her longing for Pendragon could not bring him back to her if he lay charred from the fire in a lonely grave. Fate and destiny did not concern themselves with human loves and longing, and her desires were not relevant to the path of her spiritual destiny.

The man in the dark cloak — and the Lady Ardua also, with her unexpectedly piercing and potent remarks — had succeeded in revealing to Nimue the fact that she could not accept her husband's loss. Her love for Pendragon would endure beyond the grave and transcend death, she knew, purer and finer than any love she might feel again in this life as a woman for a man. But — .

But after the wedding feast, when the players' cart had left her at her house beside the river in the early hours of the morning before lumbering off again into the dark, Nimue found herself alone in the sanctuary of her chamber trembling, unable even to think of sleep. Her whole body was vibrating with incredulous joy. Oh, could it be true and not something she herself had conjured from the force of her own desire? For she mourned her husband with every fibre of her being, and her longing for him in the flesh might, perhaps, be the instrument with which the evil one sought to overcome her — .

Whatever the cause, however it had been achieved and to what end she did not know — and she cared even less. But she was certain of one thing.

Pendragon had been with her.

Pendragon had been at the wedding feast.

She could as well mistake her own self, the breath that gave her life, as mistake what she had experienced. The touch of his hand, that long, strong hand so cruelly scarred in the earlier fire that had killed his father. She had felt it again. Somewhere among the press of dancers, she had for the fraction of a moment that blazed as an eternity now in her mind, caught her husband's hand in hers and held it.

Yes, she had taken his hand and felt its strength pass into hers, together with love that seemed to give her new hope, new life. Oh, it was true, and if this was so, then anything was indeed possible to those who trusted and had faith.

But in the end she must have slept, for there was a hand on her shoulder, rousing her, and the reaching not of a voice but of another mind into her consciousness. Nimue sat up dazedly, shaking away the veils of sleep. It was still dark, and Huw was at her bedside with a candle. Beyond, behind him, she sensed Math's presence also, like that of a changeling dark against the deeper dark. She could see the gleam of his hazel eyes.

It was Math who spoke, and Nimue was aware of a momentary stab of surprise. Math rarely spoke, and his voice had the harsh and rusty quality of something seldom used. The words he used were Welsh, but Nimue grasped their meaning immediately.

A summons — a call to Westminster —

'The Queen — ?' Nimue hazarded, her heart beginning to beat thickly in her ears, and Math spoke again. She seemed to hear the call of a bird, a lost bird that rose, soaring and swooping, freed from its confining cage to speed on the winds of home, to return to its mate. But only one word penetrated her senses.

'Pendragon.' And again. 'Pendragon.'

Nimue felt a great sense of stillness, as though she had known this moment would come, whatever it was to bring.

She had been aware since the previous evening that there were strange events afoot, deep mysteries she could not fathom. And the dark about her was swirling with the rainbow colours of magic and enchantment. Math's eyes were burning with hazel fire, and when she turned to Huw she saw the same incandescence reflected in his face. He set down the candle for her and withdrew, and Nimue did not hesitate. She scrambled out of the warmth of her bed and reached for her bodice and gown with hands that were shaking.

As she descended the stairs ready for travelling with her cloak about her, the candle held high, she saw that a man who resembled the courier the Queen had sent to summon her from Wales, was waiting. He had the same air of purpose, the same unobtrusiveness of appearance, the same directness of manner, neither that of master or servant, but of one who carried out imperatives and would brook no argument or delay. She did not recognise him, but she inclined her head, saying merely:

'I am at your disposal, sir.'

He indicated Math and Huw with a gesture.

'I am instructed to bring with you, madam, the two who accompanied you from Wales.'

And so, as though the chariot she had seen in the painted cards had materialised before her eyes, she sat within the darkened coach that had been waiting on the highway, with Huw and Math beside her, and the horses dashed them jolting off into the night.

Nimue tried to catch her breath and get her bearings as they were transported through the streets of the city. It was not yet dawn, and barely a few hours must have passed since, dazed and bemused, she had descended from the cart that had brought her home. That too had been in its way a chariot of destiny, piled high with spangles and costumes and all manner of theatrical impedimenta, that belonged to Will's company of players. After their performance at the wedding feast, they had stolen into the night like thieves, and were now, they had told her, on their way to tour the provinces.

'Here today and gone tomorrow,' Ben Ashe, who had found Nimue's grave, sweet presence an inspiration — 'a Muse' was how he had picturesquely put it — had said with a sweep of his hand, smiling down at her. And Will had of course been obliged to go with the company, but he had ensured as best he could that the girl had been brought safely home. She had been offered a horse. And 'a chariot of fire, mistress,' Benjamin Ashe had declaimed flatteringly, 'should rightfully appear whenever Beauty would travel abroad.' But the chariot of fire had not materialised, and Nimue had preferred to return with the players rather than ride, for she wanted to tell Will what had happened, to share with him the secret that was filling her being like sweet wine brimming over in a goblet.

She had clung to him at the gate of her house, where Huw stood tall in his white robes, stirred in the night wind, having emerged with a lantern to light her in. Nimue was breathless and laughing.

'Will, do you believe in miracles?'

'Would you riddle me, then, girl? Seeing the life in your eyes, the colour in your cheeks, I must believe in something,' he grinned, holding her in a loose embrace. Then, deliberately, he tilted up her chin, looking down at her face in the torchlight. 'I am overcome. What, have you declared a truce and will you love me and run away with me after all and let the world go hang?'

Blushing, Nimue pulled away, recollecting herself and her dignity, but it was difficult to keep her poise, to be cool and aloof when all her senses were vibrant and singing with joy.

'I love all the world tonight, Will,

for I have seen something I would not have believed, something that cannot be, and yet it is, something that has transformed my life for me — .'

He bent to press a quick, fond kiss on her cheek.

'Ah, is not that always the effect of a wedding, that it reduces all of womankind to mooning and making sheep's eyes? I am glad, girl, if you are in better spirits. But I must be gone, it is a long way to Bath and we would snatch some sleep before morning. I leave you in the care of your angel — .' He looked towards Huw's impassive figure. 'I would stay and debate the nature of miracles with you until dawn, but as we in the theatre put it, the show must go on, and so we must take to the road.'

'Goodbye, Will,' she told him, half-relieved that he had not given her the chance to recount what had happened at the wedding feast — for she was not certain whether she could believe it herself — and she moved towards where Huw stood at the gate.

With a swirl of his cloak, he was gone to swing himself up again onto the cart, where the other players were dozing, snatching what sleep they could amid the clutter of their trade, only the driver bent over the traces of the horse. And as though they were the products of their own illusory craft, and could perform in their sleep, Nimue thought that the sounds of a lute and the rhythmic pulse of the crumhorn lingered behind them on the night air, together with a voice that pronounced thrillingly:

'If music be the food of love, play on — .'

She strained her eyes, but they were gone into the night.

★ ★ ★

And now, as though the drum rolled to announce another play, she and Huw and Math were rumbling through the dark streets of the city, summoned by — whom? Pendragon, Math had said — . And so, did that mean — ? But Nimue did not dare to think what this summons in the deepest hour of night might mean. Her pulses were still throbbing at the recollection of that touch on her fingers during the dancing. She could not have been mistaken. But if he was alive — .

She remembered how her father had often said that there should be temperance in all things, that too much joy was as bad as too little — and she found she was smiling to herself. It was true, for she was likely to die of her joy, she thought, lifting her hands to her burning cheeks in the darkness of the coach. Could it be possible? Her husband had been burned in the fire at Pendragon — the old Druid Owain ab Owain had told her so himself, and he would not lie — .

Yet suddenly she found herself recalling that terrible night again. The words that had been said. The emotions she had previously been unable to face.

And she realised the truth.

She had not seen Pendragon's body. She had left, assured by the old man that it was better so.

'You may leave him in my care. I will do what needs to be done.'

He had known, she realised now, with utter certainty. He had known Pendragon lived. And yet he had not told her, he had let her depart for London at the Queen's command. But if her husband had escaped the fire, then where had he been and why had he not come to her? She bit her lip against the anguish that rose in her throat, swallowing hard. He was her dearest lord of dark and light. How could he have let her suffer so, believing him dead?

And if after all he had been there, last night — . Her heart contracted. If he had been there, how was it that she not seen him, recognised him? If he had been there, why had he not revealed himself, made his presence known to her?

The miracle was turning into something else now, something more sinister, and Nimue felt her colour rise and then drain from her cheeks as her thoughts moved frantically on from one question to another. She could not see the faces of Huw and Math in the darkened coach, but suddenly she wondered, with a chillness that seemed to penetrate into her very bones.

Had they too been aware that Pendragon lived? Huw surely would have known of such a momentous presence as life and death both by the magic he had been taught and by his own shining rare sense of truth. But then, why had he too kept that truth from her — ?

Elation, wonder, were followed by hurt that she should have been so duped, and a stabbing fear lest she had been mistaken in believing she could trust this scarred man, lord of a high, wild tower who spoke with angels and demons and who was yet, albeit she had married him, a stranger. But even as she felt herself begin to tremble at the thought, the coach slowed to a stop, the horses snorting, and there were low voices outside and lights visible as the heavily curtained door was pulled open.

Nimue caught her breath, feeling almost too weak from anticipation and dread to rise from her seat, but Huw's hand was beneath her elbow, and there was another arm extended by the man who was waiting to help her to descend. In the flickering torchlight, all her senses heightened, she was aware of dark walls and the brooding presence of an unsleeping force beyond them, at work while the rest of the world slumbered. Then, with Huw and Math a pace behind her, she had passed through a door and was being conducted through the halls and chambers of the great palace of Westminster. And then she stopped upon the threshold of a small room where a fire burned, and candles, and a man waited. The sight of his face transported her back to the night when she had first arrived from North Wales and she drew her breath as the realities of time blurred and merged.

'My lord Burleigh,' she said, bewildered. Had she dreamed all that had happened since that long ride in response to the Queen's summons? Was this Westminster, or was she still standing before the table in Greenwich where Burleigh was instructing her on the part she must play to discover and defeat the threat of the Hand of Glory, while Arabella Nevile, soft-footed, slipped away to where Elizabeth of England still sat in the room beyond the arras?

Burleigh came forward, moving with difficulty. He paused before her and when, uncertainly, she extended her hand he bent formally to kiss it. When he lifted his eyes to her face, she saw a flicker of unexpected emotion in his wily and withered features.

'Mistress Pendragon, Her Grace is unable to grant you an audience but she has ordered me to convey to you her great pleasure at the faithfulness and loyalty you have displayed — though no more than she expected from the wizard Gwynne's daughter — to her person and to the state.' He had recovered himself now, and only a thin smile touched his lips as he added meaningfully:

'She authorises me to restore to you that which you would most desire as an especial mark of her favour.' He turned his head. 'She gives you back your husband.'

Then Nimue almost screamed. The figure that came forward from an inner room was tall and menacing, the face concealed by its long black hair and thick beard, the form wrapped in a dark cloak and shadowed by a wide brimmed hat. Ill-omened as a raven, it bore down on her and she threw up her hands in terror, fearing that she and all of them were lost.

'It is he — the Counsellor — the Holy Devil — . It is this man who has the power — I warned Mister Cecil but oh, it is too late now — . He has bewitched you, bewitched you all,' she managed to stammer into the cold wind that seemed to blow through the chamber, chilling her to the marrow, shaking her limbs and freezing the scream on her lips.

Then out of the dark of horror and despair, Pendragon's voice seized her by the throat, mocking her, stilling her wild heart, filling her whole body with honeyed sweetness.

'Ah, witch, will you deny the spirit for the sake of the outward form?' it mourned. 'Will you cast me off because I have lost my beauty? It is cruel you are to a man who has waited days and nights and travelled a weary way to find you.'

And then, heedless of the barriers of cloak and hat and the thickness of beard and waving locks (which proved later to be false), Nimue was lifted off her feet and held close, sobbing and laughing in disbelieving joy, in her husband's arms.

'It was the power — I saw the power but I mistook the source of it,' she tried to explain breathlessly, when at last coherent speech between them became possible. 'I thought it was you — the Counsellor — the Holy Devil. But if it was not you — oh then, it must be that woman Maire Maeve — or Judith Carter — Rosalind — or even all the three of them.'

'Even so, witch,' he agreed, his face grave. 'For I am in the Queen's confidence, no enemy of the people. And the Irish Queen Granuille, at whom the finger of suspicion has also been pointed, she is a great lady, no traitor either. Oh, she would make a formidable foe, I grant you, but she is honourable. She has seen Elizabeth, and has spoken with a good heart, my Lord Burleigh will tell you. All is well there witch, it is not from the eternal ebbing and flowing of the Irish politics that this danger comes.'

'No, no,' Nimue was only half listening to what he said in the delight of hearing the tones of his voice again. But she sensed the urgency in his words, and suddenly she was recalling her vision, her dream, her flight by strange and subtle magic to the wild coast and the cliffs in the far west. She turned to Burleigh.

'Sir, I must speak with you on this matter. I have seen the source of the danger, I know now that it comes from the sea — from some vessel that is called the *Santa Catalina*. I have seen it, this ship, and seen a boat put out from it and make for the land — .'

Burleigh was staring at her, and Pendragon's eyes were very dark, very intent.

'Can it be, my lord, can it be that this ship is the link that could not be found? The way in from Spain, the means?'

Nimue watched, only half-comprehending, struggling to understand.

'Yet the shadow is cast in Ireland — .

So if it is not Madam O'Malley,' she began. Then suddenly: 'The holy sister, Maire Maeve. Is she not Irish also?'

'The woman who calls herself Maire Maeve is not Irish, Mistress Pendragon,' Burleigh's dry, toneless voice interrupted her. 'The investigations we have managed to make so far have revealed that she is of Spanish blood, and claims descent by bastardy through her mother from the royal line of Spain, from Juana the mad, after whom she was named.'

Nimue's mind was running fast, ahead of his.

'That pride, that single-minded, arrogant purpose,' she breathed in immediate understanding. 'Oh yes, I see it all now. She could not bear to be a humble instrument of God, though she told me herself that she had studied — I supposed for her religious vocation — in Rome — .'

'She entered an order noted for its austere severity but also for its un-Christian manipulation of politics, witch. Approved by none other than

Machiavelli himself, who wrote his own disreputable epitaph within the pages of his treatise *Il Principe*,' Pendragon told her, and she looked up as Lord Burleigh's measured tones added words Nimue also knew, for her father had often been challenged to dispute the merit of inspiring fear in order to gain or maintain power.

Sudents of philosophy and sometimes of alchemy, magic or even power for its own sake, had made Gereint Gwynne smile a little as they earnestly quoted Machiavelli's principles of government, his instructions to *The Prince*, which he had based it was believed, on the methods of the Borgias, particularly Cesare, son of the Borgia Pope Alexander VI.

'Is it better to be loved than feared, or the other way about? . . . it is far safer to cultivate fear . . . men love only when it suits them . . . the prince should seek only to avoid being hated.'

'They must have all known — the Druid and the Queen — and Mister Cecil — . They must have all known that you lived.' Nimue hid her face in her hands suddenly, then turned to her husband, the words surfacing in spite of herself from the depths of her confusion of swirling passions. She was quivering — she told herself it was with fury, though she knew in her heart that it was with relief at the realisation she had not lost him after all. 'If they knew, then why, oh why did you not tell me you had survived the fire? It was cruel — . I might have died of grief.'

Pendragon was sitting with a goblet of wine held easily in his hand, the long length of his body visible now that he had removed the all-concealing black cloak and the black hat. While Burleigh watched impassively, he lifted the goblet in a toast to Nimue, though she could not see his features clearly behind the all-too-concealing black beard. His eyes mocked at her, and she suspected he was actually laughing.

'*Diawl*, I would never have let you die, witch. I have been with you all the time since you came to London, watching over you — and breaking my heart that I could not reveal myself beneath my disguise. But it had to be so, for if you had not believed me gone — though that came about by fate and fortune rather than by intent — you could not have acted out your part with such sincerity. And had you thought — those three, the Spanish Dona Juana and her fellow conspirators — would they have felt they could ask you to join them if you had been a dutiful wife to your loving lord? Husbands can play no part in plots for overthrowing male domination in the world — except like Judith Carter's, they are safely in the tomb. We could never have foreseen it, witch, for we were ignorant of the nature of the Hand of Glory, but providence and the angels thought for us, and so for a time I had to die.'

'But — .' She stopped, shaking her head helplessly. It was enough that he was here, that he had come back to her from the grave — though there was nothing of the grave about him, and he seemed more alive than everyone else in the chamber, Math and Huw, Lord Burleigh, even herself.

'When they fired Pendragon,' he told her, 'I was not there. Though Pendragon is a wild place, yet it is not so wild that the servants of the great do not know the road to the tower well. Many have been the summons that have come — for my father before me, and now for me — to advise and counsel and read the charts, ask the stars and planets for guidance. At the time of the Armada, as I told you, I worked in my father's place for England — as did your own father, my witch — and the Queen sent to consult me when the others, her everyday astrologers like John Dee, could tell her no more about this latest threat — this Hand.'

Nimue listened, watching the light and shade of the candle flames play across his face, trying to see the scars beneath the thick curling black beard. The long all-concealing mop of hair (largely false), had been unceremoniously removed together with the 'Counsellor's' hat, and the hair now lay next to the wine jug on the board beside him like some lurking rodent. The beard, however, was more firmly attached to his face — some of it, indeed, his own — and he grinned cheerfully at her confusion.

'Oh, you are the wife to a man of influence my witch. The Queen had sent for me secretly, and with orders that I must not tell you or anyone, but go. I sent Huw to you to reassure you, for I would never have abandoned you for the world, and I let you see me — .'

Coming out of the sunrise, she remembered, astride Taliesin, his great white horse.

'Then the night came of the fire,' he continued. 'None knew I was in London, from home. And you — as well as those who set the torch to Pendragon — thought I was dead. That was how it was.'

Leaning forward, he touched her cheek gently with his finger as though the frozen tears of that anguish still clung and he would release them, let them flow and so wipe out the memory of the frost that had blighted her heart and petrified her soul even in the midst of the fire's heat.

'The Druid — Owain ab Owain — as you say, he knew the truth, and so did Huw and Math,' he continued sombrely, 'but they are not of this world, witch, and life or death to them is only a turning like the day and the night, the old year and the new, the tide or the phases of the moon. Besides, the Queen had by then sent for you also, before she was aware that we were wedded, and there were — .' He looked up into her eyes.

'Other matters to consider.'

'Gilbert — and the gold — and Ralph Tollaster's murder,' Nimue said in a low voice, and her husband nodded.

'We knew something of it at Pendragon, and I have since discovered the rest. We knew who took the rock, the mining sample from my father's wooden chest. I had gone before Tollaster was killed but Owain heard the truth of it and in his concern for you, he wanted you away from Wales. But we are not barbarians, and the lawyer Ruffard Rowland has gone to Flint at my request, to look into the affairs I left behind me. Owain ab Owain still faithfully stewards our estates, and matters are in hand even now. There are actions being brought concerning the enclosures, the land claims. And against those who took the law into their own hands.' He made a slight, dismissive gesture.

'The mills of man grind even more slowly than the mills of God sometimes, witch, but all will yet receive justice, whether human or divine. We must live by the laws of our society — or at any rate, seem to be seen to do so in order to inspire confidence in our people. The wrongs that are being done in the name of land enclosure, and the restrictions of civil liberties must be confronted even if there is no solving of them. I have not forgotten Gwilym the Stone, and his dead Cait and their baby — and all the others who are under the protection of Pendragon — though I am in no mind to lead a crusade. But Mister Rowland has gone to gather the necessary information to redress these matters legally — and to proceed against Stoneyathe of Grannah.'

Reassured, yet still troubled, Nimue spoke uneasily.

'It was the gold, the stone that was stolen from Pendragon tower. Ralph Tollaster taunted Gilbert with it, and then, that day when the mob went to fire Pendragon, Gilbert rode out with Mister Tollaster and killed him. I saw him — .'

'You saw him? But you told Mister Rowland you had no evidence of any man's guilt, mistress,' Burleigh interrupted in his thin tones, and Nimue turned to him. She had forgotten in her absorbtion with her husband, that they were not alone.

'I saw his eyes when they rode in with the body,' she said simply. 'His guilt was plainly written there — and he was holding the stone, the sample of gold, in his hands.'

Burleigh gave the slightest of shrugs. He had withdrawn into a polite, discreet silence while the first breathless words were said, the first questions half-spoken, half-answered, but now he seemed to re-establish his control of the gathering in the chamber, and spoke with authority.

'The death of this man — Stoneyathe's bailiff — has been accepted as an unfortunate and tragic accident. There was no evidence, no proof of murder. The dead man, Mistress Pendragon, apparently fell some distance and died of internal injuries, that is what the medical man who attended the body has testified. Under oath.' As Nimue drew in her breath to protest, he gave her a look that spoke eloquently.

'The events in question on this occasion seem to have been irregular in the extreme. Investigations have also been made into allegations of — .' He paused, then said: 'Witchcraft. A capital offence, Mistress Pendragon.'

The girl froze, dismayed, remembering suddenly those vicious, spiteful accusations Mary and Dorabella had hurled at her across Ralph Tollaster's body, adding their voices to Gilbert's. For a moment the cold grip of fear — fear of the mindless violence of the mob as it rumbled to itself like a summer storm gathering — seized her again, and Burleigh saw her eyes.

'You are accused of nothing, Mistress Pendragon,' he said more gently. 'Any allegations that were made against you have been withdrawn. There is no case to answer. And — .' He made a slight movement of his hand. 'The bailiff has been buried — at the expense of his lord, Stoneyathe of Grannah — and his death has been recorded as an accident.' His voice fell so low she could hardly hear it.

'It would, perhaps, be wise to let matters rest there and pursue them no further.'

Nimue, thus appealed to, nevertheless wanted to protest. Gilbert Stoneyathe had killed in cold blood, deliberately taken the life of another human being. But then she saw her husband watching her. His voice seemed to whisper in her mind, though he did not speak.

'All will have justice, whether human or divine, my witch. Gilbert Stoneyathe has killed and he must sooner or later face a greater than the circuit judge. None can escape the laws nor the hand of God.'

She hesitated. She had no evidence, it was true, only her own intuitive certainty of Gilbert's guilt. But even though he might congratulate himself that he was free, in the end he would not be able to run from the consequences of his action. And in the end too, it was not after all she who must take the responsibility for administering his punishment. She had done what she could, and must leave the rest to God. But in the meantime — .

'I think you will find that Mister Stoneyathe has had a shock,' Lord Burleigh commented drily, still watching her. 'He has found, perhaps for the first time in his life, that responsibility and power carry with them their own safeguards — notoriety and the close attention of others. His actions will find him out, and regarding his estates, as he seeks to force the courts of law to grant him permission to do as he chooses, he is about to discover that justice in this land is for all, and the law also upholds the rights of others. There will be legal battles that will drag on for years in England, mark me, Mistress Pendragon, to establish

320

the rights to the lands that he — and others, too many of them — have enclosed, and Mister Stoneyathe will find in the future that his every action will be under scrutiny. For Wales,' he added pointedly, 'is no far-flung continent, but a part of England.'

Pendragon, lord of a tower whose laws were written in winds and waters, looked at Nimue with a world of far-flung continents in his eyes, so that she almost laughed aloud, but he said nothing. And neither did she. They would not speak of these things again, for a chapter had, however surreptitiously and cautiously, closed.

10

And now it was May Eve, and Nimue stood with Huw and Math beneath a racing, cloud-racked sky. Night was drawing in over the huge circle of silent stones that crouched, yet towered before them. The contours of the land swept emptily away on each side, and the lost place vibrated with awful mystery. It was filled with power and magic. Stonehenge, people called it.

Pendragon had sent her here, instructing her to ride fast and alone, attended only by Huw and Math in order that she might fight the last, the final battle with the woman from Spain who would overthrow the order and peace of all the kingdom. It was there, he had told her, that she could call on the strongest, the most secret and awesome power of the earth, for this was a sacred place and one that had been old long before the most ancient of earthly gods had lived.

'They say it was the Druids that raised the stones to worship the sun, but it was not so,' he had said quietly. 'They have always been there, and the faithful borrow them only — these and other such circles — for their rites. But go you, witch, for the stones will keep themselves for you alone on this night of Beltane, and you shall kindle such a fire as will purge this land of all trace of Spanish infiltration, and rid men's minds of what Dona Juana and her kind have planted, and would plant there, root and branch.'

★ ★ ★

As she rode with Huw and Math through the land in its April green, deeper into the secret places where no bird sang for reverence, Nimue had had time to think, to ponder on all the subtleties — and yet, the amazing simplicity — of the Spanish plot, the truth of the Hand of Glory. In the end, as Burleigh had charged her at the beginning, it was to be herself, young and as yet untried, who must face the threat of the Hand alone, and overcome it. For as Pendragon had reminded her, the things of the dark may only be defeated by their other selves, their forms of light. A woman was at the heart of the conspiracy, a woman who used her religion to justify and further her own prideful desires and arrogant ends, and so it must be another woman who must vanquish her by testing and proving by her own faithfulness, even beyond death if it had to be so, the emptiness of her spiritual weapons.

The revolution, the seeds of the revolt which might have brought England beneath the boot of Spain — and still would if she failed, for the danger was not yet over — had proved to be both the spiritual threat she had sensed intuitively, and also an affair of political motivation, something of both the worlds, the world of the body and the world of the soul. Burleigh's agents had worked fast once they were given the link with Dona Juana, a supposed Irish religious whose fervours had been cunningly adapted by the dispassionate power-lords of Spain to conquer in the name of Castile and Aragon rather than of God.

'A religious order — well, it may be,' Lord Burleigh had said of the organisation to which Dona Juana Sant'Anna had pledged herself. She had assumed the more humble robe and name of the holy sister 'Maire Maeve' in order, it now appeared, to ingratiate herself with women like Rosalind Blackcross and Judith Carter — and other like-minded feminist obsessionists, of spiritual power and influence (whether real or assumed) whose minds she could inflame. 'But its roots lie deep in politics and in power. Power on the scale that Niccolo Machiavelli himself never dreamed of, Mistress Pendragon. Extreme power for the sake of domination, of complete repression. There is no tolerance, no charity, no place for any except the chosen few in this order — and they appoint themselves.'

Nimue nodded slowly. She was realising that her intuition, her inner vision, had not played her false.

'They all — the three of them — spoke of power. They promised me power, also. Even Rosalind Blackcross, who came to me first, described my father as powerful rather than a man of goodness or holiness. And — .' She spoke without being aware, her gaze turning inward, remembering that the signs had been there from the start, if she had had the wit to see them.

'Rosalind Blackcross wore an amulet, a stone that she said she used to invoke the Hand — . It was an amethyst. A beautiful stone, but as my father taught me, its imperial purple is the colour of majesty and power — . Again, power.'

Pendragon looked across at her, his eyes shadowed.

'She is young, my witch, it is true. Yet she chose freely to welcome the tempter who offers us all the riches of this world at the price of our souls. She had a mother who had done the same — .'

'Jemima Blackcross,' Nimue murmured, understanding all now, save that she suddenly roused herself from her thoughts. 'She came to my father at the end, but how did you know that?'

He smiled, the sombreness lifting.

'My familiar, the Lady Ardua. The girl speaks sometimes to those she trusts — and Ardua has very large ears.'

Nimue was silenced, her attention diverted from Rosalind Blackcross, the child who had yet chosen when she was old enough to choose, to share the cloud of corruption and the black arts which Nimue had seen around her mother. That same mother who, Gereint Gwynne had mourned, had taken a path she had later regretted.

Nimue opened her mouth to speak,

then shut it. She had not had time to consider the implications of her husband's impersonation of some kind of Puritan kill-joy, an evangelist who would rearrange the lives and pleasures of others for his own gloomy satisfaction. And she had certainly not had time to form a new opinion about the Lady Ardua, who if she recollected rightly, had for some time been sharing a parlour with her mentor, the 'Counsellor'.

But though objectionably direct and forceful in her speech, and though resembling one of the more vigorous characters from a mumming play in her dress, the Lady Ardua was a female and apparently a woman of means — of breeding, too, Nimue remembered rather dazedly. She would have bitten off her tongue rather than asked, but she could not help burning with unworthy curiosity as to the relationship between her husband and this colourful personality.

Pendragon, amused, was watching

her mental struggles as she tried to keep silent. Then he told her smiling:

'The agents of the crown come in many strange guises, witch. I was a reluctant spy, see you, and not accustomed to the streets of the city, but for those weeks when I was first in London trying to discover the secrets of the Hand, I needed to be able to move about freely — as you did yourself with Mister Shakespeare. The Lady Ardua was my guide — and as my acolyte and follower, a necessary part of my disguise as the Counsellor. A gentlewoman she is, whose place should be at home nodding beside the hearth or bouncing her grandchildren upon her bony knees and preaching to them, whose duty is to suffer her, rather than to those who owe her no such duty. But she will not have it. Her husband was a soldier who died in the cause of his country, and she threw off her shackles of respectable widowhood at his death and took up the torch that had fallen from his hand. In the best way she could, though tongues wagged. She serves where she might be helpful.' He paused, then his voice softened in much the same way that Robert Cecil's had done when he spoke of Ardua.

'A great, a very great lady witch, for all that there is little comfort for a man in her company — even one like myself who can command the elements — since it is impossible to command her tongue, which is as sharp as a thistle.'

At his recollected ruefulness Nimue found herself laughing, but Lord Burleigh's precise tones recalled her to the reality of the situation.

'The Lady Ardua poses as an eccentric to give myself and Sir Francis Walsingham intelligence that may assist the state,' he said, as though reluctant to part with the information, and she inclined her head to indicate that she would respect his confidence. 'She assisted your husband to watch over you and give you what protection we could, Mistress Pendragon. And also, since his ways are somewhat unworldly, we appointed her to watch over him,' he added pointedly, and an expression of comical dismay flickered across Pendragon's scarred face. Burleigh, unaware, continued to inform Nimue.

'All that you did was reported to me, though not, inevitably, all that you might have said — nor all that was said to you. And in spite of my son's opinion that the letter you received from Dame Judith Carter would prove of little significance, you were followed even to Mister Jobling's at Chelsea, though even I, I admit, had no suspicion that he was any threat.'

Considering the portly pompousness of the merchant, his unctious desire to please and ingratiate, and the way Judith Carter had spoken of him and treated him, Nimue said slowly:

'Mister Jobling is their tool. I think they would make all men so.'

'There are many sour females — whether with reason or without it — who hate men,' Burleigh nodded.

'Or perhaps, hate other women, my lord,' Pendragon said, soft as a thought, and once more Nimue saw the eyes of Mary and Dorabella as they had thrown their accusations of witchcraft across the torchlit yard at Grannah. And heard the shrieks of the crowd as the young widow in Southwark stumbled, wild-eyed and lost, with her children beneath their baying and baiting.

The words of the three women at Chelsea slithered, insinuating as snakes, through her consciousness.

'We believe that women, not men should rule in the world.'

Oh, she could see now that she had been blind not to realise that the sorceresses had told her their whole intent, the whole of their proposed undertaking, in those few words. No need indeed for an army, for booted Spanish soldiers to tread the streets of London. Nor even for black magicians with the powers of a magus to spin their webs of darkness to shroud their sinister doings.

She could understand now why she had felt such unease when she had looked at the painted card of a veiled, secretive woman in the pack that had been her father's. Feeding, gorging itself on the ambitions of others, there had indeed been one mind of towering personal arrogance which had blocked the vision of enquirers into the significance of the Hand of Glory. But it had not been that of some great magician skilled in demonic lore. It had been the mind that hid itself behind the mask of a holy sister, an apparent daughter of the church, one who wore a cross upon her breast and the plain robe of an ascetic who had renounced the world upon her back.

It was Dona Juana Sant' Anna who had provided the real threat to England and to Englishmen — a threat that might have enslaved their bodies and damned their souls. She had skilfully concealed the extent of her real self, that self which could never be humble. And because her religion and the practise of it had made her strong, so when she turned from grace her dark strength too was as formidable as that of any practitioner of the black arts.

★ ★ ★

Within the chamber at Westminster, many things were made clear.

'Regarding Ireland,' Burleigh had pursued with deliberation. 'Your information was of inestimable value, Mistress Pendragon, and on receipt of your reports I was able to order that immediate enquiries were set in motion. I questioned the Irish lady, Grainne O'Malley myself, and she told me — with the aid of an interpreter of the Irish tongue, for her Latin is somewhat lacking — that she had recognised you as a wild female, a supposed witch who wanders the shores of what they call in that country, Liscannor Bay and who is sometimes to be seen near the cliffs where there is an ancient stronghold, Moher.'

As they listened, Pendragon's fingers closed round those of his wife, but neither of them spoke.

'It appears,' Burleigh continued emotionlessly, 'that the female in question was some sort of foundling who was taken to the abbey at Ennis, and placed in the care of holy nuns. But she was wild — and she suffered from fits where she would fall like one dead to the ground, but come to herself afterwards and speak of wonders and visions. The people shunned her, and she ran away to live alone beside the sea. They call her Nemah in the Irish tongue, and believe she consorts with spirits, I understand.'

He paused, and there was silence in the chamber. Nimue's skin prickled cold, though the April night was balmy and there was a fire burning. This was too great a mystery for her even to begin to question it.

'I sent dispatches to Ireland, and this woman was apprehended by government officers, with a view to questioning her,'

Burleigh continued. He was watching Nimue closely. 'But when the officers went to the cell where she had been confined, there was — .' And he shrugged slightly. 'No-one to be found.'

Pendragon's hand tightened on Nimue's.

'She had escaped?'

'She had — gone. That much is certain. The cell was empty. The door was still closely locked and guarded. The woman had vanished. No-one saw her go — and no-one has seen her since.'

There was another silence. Nimue was aware that all in the chamber were looking to her, and she spoke as composedly as she could.

'If you want answers, my lord, I can give you none. I know nothing of this woman, nor of her escape from a locked cell. All I can tell you is that I have experienced visions — dreams — myself, where I seemed to be standing at the edge of the far ocean, where the cliffs and the shore you have described must lie. And I have seen — whether through the eyes of another or through my own, I do not know — but I have seen a ship, as I told you, a ship with its sails furled standing off the coast and from it, a boat putting out to the land. The *Santa Catalina*.'

'The means by which the Spanish woman entered Ireland?,' Burleigh murmured thoughtfully.

'At first, I mistook the visions I was given, my lord,' Nimue told him, her face intent with concentration as she tried to make him understand — and to understand herself. She gave a slight, dismissive gesture. 'It can happen so when the images are not clear. I told you when first we spoke of the Hand that there was some dark magic, some strong imposed will that blocked the vision. All those you consulted saw the same. But I did not recognise, even when I saw her, that it was Dona Juana — Maire Maeve.

I thought instead it must be the Holy Devil — not recognising my husband in his disguise — for I feared the strength of the power he had over me — .'

She tried to maintain an even tone, though Pendragon's eyes were openly mocking her. She clasped her hands together, striving for dignity.

'I thought at first that it must be he who was the enemy, and when Rosalind Blackcross came to me — my lord, I even began to wonder whether she had come as an ally, to help me. Even when we spoke in Chelsea and I met the others, I could not be sure — .'

She shrugged a little, ruefully, and Burleigh nodded with unexpected understanding.

'The situation was never clear, Mistress Pendragon, if it had been there would have been no need for you to risk yourself in order to discover the truth for us. We anticipated that it would not be easy for you and even that you might be placed in danger.

You will recollect that I warned you of the risks at the beginning. However,' he smiled thinly, 'you were never alone. Your husband has been your shadow since you arrived in London.'

Nimue exclaimed in confusion, still not able to believe it, and Pendragon leaned across to her, his voice deepening.

'Closer I have been to you than even your own shadow,' he told her huskily. 'Once we knew you were coming, that you had left Wales after the fire and Owain had sent you into my keeping, I did not leave your side, my witch. Do you recall that other shadow that caused the little dog to bark in the gallery at Chelsea?'

She froze, feeling again the tension in the air as the women demanded whether she would join with them, and the curious paralysis that seemed to have descended on her, the heaviness of her neck and head, the way she had — helplessly — been about to answer them. And then, the movement at the window and the little dog running from

Judith Carter's skirts, yapping shrilly.

'The bird — it was you — ?'

'It was indeed a bird — yet not there by chance. I sent it, witch. You would have given yourself into their power if something had not distracted you, woken you from your sleeping. For do you not know that evil can only harm you if it is permitted to enter, welcomed in? Bar it entry, and it cannot touch your soul.'

She smiled despite the seriousness of it, seized with a sudden imp of mischief.

'I learned that at my father's knee. Oh, but indeed I see the truth now. You were jealous and needed some excuse to play the spy upon me, that is all. Did you not trust me in the company of my dear Will, my father's old friend? For shame, my lord, for shame.'

His black gaze sparked a mocking challenge at her.

'True it is that a thankless child is sharper than a serpent's tooth,' he

340

intoned piously in the voice of the 'Counsellor'. 'And a thankless wife even worse than that. And — .' Turning. ' — here is the woman who will bear me witness that I speak the right of it.'

And then, as though it was the most natural thing in the world, a tall figure materialised through the inner door like a decked Maypole, wearing the purple farthingale and mantilla Nimue had seen the evening before at the wedding feast. Jet and black crystal winked like dark, erratic stars on a frosty night.

'Mistress Pendragon. I see,' said the Lady Ardua, fixing Nimue with a stare from her piercing eyes, 'that you have had the sense to take my advice. And very properly, for a husband will effectively cure you of all your unfortunate tendencies to megrims and mopery. Be grateful, child, that the Counsellor's zeal is such that he is prepared to overlook your baser attributes — far too many for a man of such fastidious thrift — in his appreciation of what there might be in your soul.'

In the sudden stillness, all eyes went to Nimue's face. The girl did not see them, for she was staring at something in Lady Ardua's expression that had meaning for her alone. Then she said, with a little indrawn breath:

'Madam, I will.'

* * *

The great stone circle held power that touched Nimue as soon as she set her eyes on it. There was a sound, a low humming beneath the surface of her inner consciousness that made her think some great beast waited, held in check there. And though the day was fair, the wind sweeping in mad bursts over the curves of the land that lifted itself slightly on each horizon, dancing madcap April madness, yet it seemed to cease deliberately as they approached and there was a stillness she could almost have touched.

As she viewed the stones, siting her mare next to Huw, Nimue saw that the green turf about their feet was green no longer. The scene was etched in black and white. There was snow on the ground, a hard frost, and figures in long robes moved purposefully about. Monks, she wondered? Then, in the flicker of an eye there was nothing but the empty turf and the silence and the wind gusting.

Yet though the vision had gone, she was still aware of the great power leashed in that place, and she understood why Pendragon had sent her here. This was one of the doorways to the Otherworld, one of the gateways into the past and future time. Nothing could take place lightly here, whatever happened must be charged with portent and significance.

'What must I do?' she had asked Pendragon, when at last the time had come to make plans. Burleigh and the Lady Ardua were watching them, while Huw and Math waited silently at the edge of the group, but her husband placed his hands on her shoulders and spoke as though they were alone, standing in the quiet chamber in Pendragon tower where the starry globe of the heavens had lain shimmering before them.

'As to that, witch, I do not know, save that you be there and be ready. This woman, and women like her would do a more subtle wrong than to enslave men and bring them to their knees. They would seek to alter the balance of life itself, and reduce men to lesser beings while they become inflated with greatness that is not in them. Was it not this fear that you say you saw in the eyes of the lad who brought you the summons from Judith Carter, in the eyes of Will Shakespeare? For is this not the hidden secret of the Hand of Glory — that it is not the hand of a dead man who has died on the gibbet, to burn and invoke sleep so that the honest may be robbed, but the arrogance of women who would blind the eyes of all men to what they truly are, and rob them of equality in the sight of God?'

Nimue nodded, her eyes charged with understanding.

'The lad who brought the message, I could not understand why he was afraid, for he seemed to know nothing of the Hand of Glory — .'

'No-one would have known,' Pendragon agreed, while Burleigh nodded in quick appreciation of the situation. 'What is there to know? What is there to see? The deepest threats are not the ones men can understand, threats of foreign power, of invasion, but like the creeping contagion of the plague, invisible to mortal eyes, yet ever-present and dangerous to life itself.'

'You think they seek to go that far?' Burleigh demanded, whitely, and Pendragon spread his hand.

'They will not need to do it. If they poison the minds of enough women, they can infiltrate every town, every village in the country, and no Spanish foot be set on English soil.'

They looked at each other, the same thought in every mind.

'There are cunning women in every community, every little cluster of cottages in the land,' Burleigh's voice expressed it. 'Supposed witches and sorceresses — many of them truly wise, but too many with the love of power that would make them easy prey to Dona Juana's persuasions.'

'A little skill with magic — misused, with intent to do it — and men might be kept by charms and other methods of duress in a state of living death.' Pendragon spoke the unbelievable words aloud. 'There are those with the knowledge in places beyond the seas — men of Huw's dark race, some of them — who can call the un-dead from their rest to work and slave mindlessly with no will of their own, no promise of salvation for their souls.'

'Yes, I have seen it too,' Nimue said, low, as Burleigh made a sound of

346

protest. 'I could not understand what it signified — that the true threat was not political, no revolt or revolution against the crown, but concerned with faith, with bigotry and intolerance springing from spiritual arrogance, spiritual pride. And that the most terrible danger is not to the body but to the soul — if it should be alienated from God.'

'Love alone is the weapon by which fear and evil can be vanquished,' Pendragon said to Nimue, and once again they might have been alone. 'And faith can defeat faith. Will you go for me, my lady, while I remain as I must to keep watch on this woman and her fellow sorceresses? Will you for the sake of the love that there is between us, undertake what must for all our sakes be the last struggle, and by your own trust and faith in me and in God, meet her face to face, in single combat?'

She did not need to answer, but for the sake of Burleigh and the Lady Ardua, she said in a low voice:

'In your name, my dear lord, and in the name of God, I will do it. Not by magic and charms, but by faith, trust and love.'

'Amen,' pronounced Lady Ardua vigorously, as she had done on the previous occasion when the Counsellor, the Holy Devil, had spoken to Nimue in the rain, but this time the girl did not hear her. She was looking into her husband's face.

His hands, his long lean hands with their twisted scars closed over hers.

'You are yet Maiden, Lady and guardian of the secrets of Wyrd, and thus empowered three-fold, my witch. You must ride with Huw and Math to a place that will lend you even greater power to defeat this woman, and there make your fire on May Eve, the night of Beltane when man and woman are equal. And in your name and mine, you must invoke both the goddess and her consort, the green man of the earth, to uphold the balance that is in all things.'

She did not hesitate, but raised his hands to her lips and kissed them, her eyes still brilliant upon his.

'I will go.'

★ ★ ★

It had wanted two days to the night of Beltane when they reached the stones, but she was glad they had come in good time so that she — and Huw and Math — could make preparation. She did not know what form the battle would take, but she would be there and she would be ready. She could do no more.

The stones were empty, the wind moving among them yet without moving, and voices that could not be heard repeating words that had no form. The three of them kept a vigil in turns, the men taking the watches during the dark hours while Nimue slept wrapped in her furs and thick warm cloak. Huw and Math, both deep in magic, made their own preparations, and Nimue strengthened her resolve in silent contemplation of the great Mysteries, offering herself as a path by means of which the light might redress the balance between man and woman.

Sacrifices were sometimes necessary to appease the fates, and though her dear lord had returned to her, lifting her from the depths of a dark abyss, she must trust even as far as the door to death itself. So, in prayer and meditation, she gave herself and all who looked to her to save them, into the care of the spirit that dwelt beyond space and time, and waited until the night of Beltane closed about the stones and the moment came.

★ ★ ★

In rituals as old as time, the shadows moved. The maiden in her white robe gathered the nine woods and mosses and bare-footed, knelt to kindle the need-fire that would flame the world into being and bring back the spring. The spark glowed and the maiden bent to touch the new wood while the earth waited, breath held, suspended — .

And she had been thrown forward — and backward — by the whirlwind, her senses lost, reeling — .

There was a battle raging, certainly, but was it at Harfleur — or Agincourt, or in some other place? There were cannon roaring, and the sound of drum, and she could not see for the acrid smoke. Dying men and horses were screaming in their agony, but her ears were too filled with other sounds to hear them, and the flashes of red fire and lightning that streaked down from the heavens, with its starry cosmos painted in blue and gold, blurred her eyes.

The groundlings cried 'Mercy' and 'Vengeance'. The players postured and beat their kettledrums to drown the shrieks of the dying. The fate of a kingdom was in the balance.

Nimue had heard Will Shakespeare tell her father, when they spoke of history, that in his view — as the creator of a play — any great battle, whether it had been played out on the field of Agincourt — Bosworth — or anywhere else, did not need to be portrayed as anything other than itself, for in such events was contained the whole drama of human existence.

'There are moments when the pivot shifts, when each man challenges his fate and the gods,' he had said, frowning. 'A life — a kingdom — does the outcome make any difference? The loss of honour may outweigh the loss of a crown. Yet the people do not understand this, and need the show. So let them have the king stripped and bare across the saddlebow of a common soldier from the ranks, or else standing triumphant while a *Te Deum* peals out above his head. The moment is all.'

Agincourt — and its precurser Harfleur — had been such moments, when the flower of French and English chivalry were sacrificed to bring the English Henry to a *Te Deum* in a great cathedral of France, and a Valois Princess to his bed as his bride and Queen. Then the cartographers redrew the maps of Europe. Yet why then, Nimue wondered, dazed and groping in her thoughts, was she conscious only of space and grey half-light all around her, sand gritty and wet beneath her bare feet, and the wood of the holy cross that had come from the heat of Jerusalem burning against her palms?

Benjamin Ashe's voice declaimed thunderously, and the ringing silver tones of Richard Burbage, a trumpet which might have roused armies of dead men to follow him into battle once again, echoed in Nimue's ears.

'Cry God for Harry — England — and Saint George — .'

But the boat from the *Santa Catalina* was almost beached on the wide sands of the bay, and the Spanish woman in her black cloak was almost ashore. Nimue stepped forward resolutely, her feet splashing into the spreading foam, holding up the cross, while the torch in

Math's hand smoked in long streamers of flame and darkness into the wind that came from the east, and the dawn. And Huw lifted his hands.

* * *

Voices screaming, cursing in Spanish. The woman's eyes sparking off terrors, demonic shapes forming in the clouds. Cannon and smoke.

She held fast to the wood of the holy cross, and found she was calling, but in this moment of terror, not to some great divine power, but to Pendragon. And not for him to come and save her, but to warn him, to bid him defend himself.

Muskets cracked. A strange low moan, a bubbling sound, came from Huw's lips, and she saw him fall, easily as an old, withered leaf that drops from the bough. And then Nimue forgot the fate of Elizabeth's kingdom, and the hundreds of Englishmen and their goodwives, solemn-faced children clinging to their skirts, the ordinary, the simple people who went about their days in trust and faith in their prince, in the order of things, and in God. Nimue had a sudden vision of a small dark-skinned child who had been dragged, screaming, from his mother's arms, and chained by the slave-masters in a long line of others, to walk endless days beneath a blazing sun until all sensation was lost, all terror passed — only for it to be revived beneath the knife that had cut away his manhood and the tongue that would have screamed his pain and anguish to the dark lost gods who had forsaken him.

Huw had been plucked from the waves off the cold northern coast of Wales by Pendragon's father, the old wizard. He had been nameless then, and already, at a few years old, ancient in suffering. And he had lived the rest of his days at Pendragon tower, having passed the boundaries of his scarred body, in the purity and wisdom of the spirit. He needed no tongue, for he could speak with the mind, and he had long since left forgiveness and compassion for the butchers who had wielded the knife upon his small body, behind him and passed to the plane where emotions wither to nothing in the light of awareness that all is as it must be.

But as she saw him fall, Nimue lost her sense of destiny, of higher responsibilities, and her anger and grief came, raging, to blot out her vision with white-hot fury. Was this saintly, holy man who had lived outcast from his own people, his very identity lost and mutilated by the world, whose watchwords were wisdom and serenity, to be the first victim of the Spanish woman's monstrous arrogance? Nimue forgot that her father would have counselled detachment, advised her to accept that all must perish.

If Huw had gone, then the slaughter had begun, but it must be stopped. She would die rather than let Math, or Pendragon, or any of the helpless — fathers and lovers, brothers and sons — who knew nothing of magic and could not defend themselves, be touched. Dona Juana should never set foot on the sand of Ireland, nor take one step that would bring her within sight of the English shore. She should never reach the streets of London.

Screaming, the girl plunged deeper into the spreading foam at the water's edge, where the sailors were steadying the boat with their long oars. The colours of Spain, red and gold, glowed richly and the light darted from the barrels of muskets. The Spanish woman was balanced between sand and sea and sky, with black storm clouds gathered like monsters behind her head and her outstretched hand on which an intaglio ruby flashed imperial, the sheen of blood. At her breast, a huge gold crucifix inlaid with amethysts blazed with the purple of power.

Advancing steadfastly, Nimue held out her only weapon, the little wooden cross. It seemed paltry against such might, but it had been brought by pilgrims from the holy city of Jerusalem, Pendragon had told her, and was sanctified by centuries of prayer. Simple and humble, part of the earth in its plainness of bare wood, it was no match for the shining work of human hands that swung at the Spanish woman's breast, which her twisted scream of cold fury made a mock of what she professed to honour.

Seeing the cross, the woman struck viciously at it. The girl saw it break in two, and the pieces, knocked from her hands, were lost in the swirling water. The woman was laughing triumphantly, as she turned to call the musketeers in the stern of the boat to open fire, and her shriek and the shrieking of the storm, wild with wind and waters, filled Nimue's ears.

She shut her eyes, trying to hold fast to the light that she could see streaming down from heaven, like a long finger piercing the blackness of the storm clouds. There was a crash as though the earth split open, and the smell of burning flesh and sulphur, and Nimue sank to her knees in the water, beyond fear now, beyond terror. If this was to be the end — if after all it was God's will that she must fail — .

'So be it.' She forced the murmur out through chattering teeth, through the stinging of salt spray on her lips, the force of the waves that had her, and she tried to compose herself for death.

★ ★ ★

But if she was dead and in heaven — or hell, because she was burning as though her body was on fire, and demons were prodding her with their pitchforks and shrieking with mirth as they did to the damned souls in the Miracle Plays she had laughed and cried at with Gereint Gwynne when they had both lived — then Huw had come with her. The demons danced, and the sounds went on and on, beating in her head, but Huw was holding her fast in the eye of the storm, and there was light, though she could not see it, and an easing of all conscious feeling and thought and then, a long stillness.

'You mean, I was struck by lightning at the stone circle?' she asked falteringly afterwards, when it was all faded into shredded dark cobwebs that the wind of time would disperse, and there was no more striving to be done, for the shadows had gone.

'We will never know what happened to you, my witch, and it does not matter now, for all my concern is that you are safe and I can hold you again in my arms,' Pendragon breathed fervently, and continued to growl his imprecations of thankfulness into the softness of her hair while he held her close.

'Do not ask questions of a merciful providence,' he continued after a moment, when he had regained control of himself. 'It is enough that you have survived.'

'Huw too,' she said slowly, considering now she could take time for the luxury of thinking. 'For he was with me on that shore of Ireland, and Math was there too, with a torch. And I thought Huw fell — killed, shot, and it was that which gave me the courage to feel anger and go forward — .'

'Shot, is it?' Pendragon said, hardly listening. For Huw, and all of them, were unharmed.

But it had been Huw who had held the distraught girl as the sudden storm across the Salisbury Plain had raged so heavily that the beating rain almost extinguished the flames of the Beltane fire; Huw who had lifted her when she had cried out, a terrible cry, and fallen writhing to the ground. With Math's assistance, Huw had tended her with skills only he knew, soothing the fever that had shaken her with his ancient remedies, and calling on gods who were dark like himself, to bring her back from the half-world where she had gone. It had been Huw who had carried her in his arms, weak and still dazed from the struggle, to lay her in her own bed in her chamber that looked over the garden and the river, after the long, weary journey home. Since then, Pendragon had not left her side.

'No-one was shot, witch,' he told her now. 'And the lightning did not touch you. It struck the ground.' But she shook her head, recalling the smell of sulphur, brimstone and — most terrible of all — seared, burning flesh.

'It struck — her,' she said, in a very small voice. 'I saw it reach out from the clouds like the finger of God. After she dashed the cross from my hand.' And, overcome, she buried her face in her husband's shoulder.

He too was silent at the awfulness of it, then he said:

'I spoke to Mistress Carter and the girl, Rosalind. They are women who have seen more than they thought to see, and they have been badly frightened. Indeed, Mistress Carter babbled somewhat incoherently of leaving England altogether — travelling on the continent for her health it is, witch — and the girl is to go with her as her companion. For Burleigh will watch them like a hawk else. And Mister Jobling too, but he has earnestly foresworn meddling with magic — or politics — or women, and has vowed to live celibate and inoffensive in the future, for he swears it needs a stronger stomach than his.'

After a moment, he added: 'And as for the Spanish woman — she has gone. Her bed is empty, her few possessions taken, all trace of her removed as though she had never been. No-one saw her leave, but some of the maids at Mister Jobling's, where she was lodged, speak of thunder on May Eve, and the house shaking and a black beast that ran, crashing and howling, through the yard. They say it was the devil, disguised.'

For a moment, Nimue stared at him, then she said with deliberation:

'Superstitious nonsense, my lord.'

'That,' he assured her gravely, 'was exactly what I told them myself.'

11

The Queen's face was shadowed. Deliberately, it seemed, she did not look at the two who stood before her.

'Your father — .' A skinny bejewelled finger was pointed in the direction of Pendragon. 'He was a wizard skilled in magic. Alchemy. The concepts of eternal youth and life.'

'He was not an alchemist, madam, though he knew the principles of alchemy.'

'Yet — .' Her voice was suddenly sharp. 'He, and all who claim to understand the secrets of eternal youth and life, it seems that they must still all come to the grave in the end.'

Pendragon waited for a moment, weighing his words, then he said:

'Madam, there are no secrets, only truths beyond the comprehension of our human minds. And the grave — .'

'Do not preach to me, Mister Pendragon, I hear enough preaching from my bishops, whose business it is to reassure me that my soul will be saved and wafted to realms celestial when I die,' she snapped irritably. 'The Almighty and I are old friends, and I have diced with him for my life many times, and come to know the cold claw of death well. And yet, for all of that, sir, I am still here, and still living, and I cannot think that I will enjoy any pleasures in heaven better than those I have savoured here on the earth.'

While Nimue, standing dutifully beside her husband, waited, wondering, the Queen seemed to debate with herself. Then she continued:

'But I have heard of a man — an alchemist — Nicolas Flamel by name —.'

She paused interrogatively. In the silence, the candle flames limned Pendragon's scarred face so that he looked suddenly stern, like some judge who must pronounce sentence. But when he spoke, there was gentleness, as well as finality, in his voice.

'Your Grace, you are a sovereign lady who holds the power of life and death, yet it is all illusory, and you know this is so. There is no elixir of life, no eternal youth save in the other world to which all, not those who can fuse the metals into the silver and the gold, will pass. True wisdom recognises no power of life save that granted by God, and withdrawn by him when the time comes.'

'He has been seen,' declared the Queen, uncompromisingly. 'This man, this Nicolas Flamel. He has been seen, and so has his wife. Walking the streets of Paris, seventy years after they were buried by the rites of the holy church. And more — . It is known that he actually achieved the mastery and succeeded in transmuting base metals into gold. Treasure beyond price. Pure gold. I have read the testimony of witnesses, reputable witnesses. If this is so — .'

Gold! Nimue's thoughts went to the wild mountain in the west, Pendragon land, where somewhere, as her visions had revealed to her, the precious metal lay waiting to be mined. It was for the sake of the small rock threaded with veins of yellow-red, the fire that blazed in the light and enflamed the passions of men, that Ralph Tollaster had met his death, and Gilbert Stoneyathe, who had murdered him, had forfeited his immortal soul. Nimue's heart swelled suddenly with a kind of desperation.

Was it always so? Was there no-one, even a woman with the worldly wisdom of a lifetime as girl child of a king, herself a princess and a Queen, who was free of the gold fever? It was no wonder that the old wizard Pendragon had hesitated until the moment of his death before he had revealed the secret of the Pendragon gold to his son.

Anguished, she glanced at the scarred face of the man beside her. Pendragon was silent for so long that the Queen, herself skilled in the arts of persuasion by words, relinquished her own advantage and spoke at random. Her voice was low.

'I am an old woman,' she said. 'My span on this earth is almost measured. Do not mistake me, Mister Pendragon, I do not delude myself that my own desire is sufficient to justify renewed life. But I am a prince, and my country has need of me. If I could ensure only a few years more — time to do more for those who look to me for their security, their peace, their right to sleep peacefully in their beds.'

'So men have argued throughout the centuries, madam. Yet somehow, the world continues to survive. Nature will not tolerate a hole, and makes sure all gaps are filled. There is no-one and nothing that is not expendable,' Pendragon dared to say drily, and Nimue's heart beat with sudden alarm at the expression that crossed the Queen's face. Then, Elizabeth laughed.

'So much trouble as the Welsh Arthur must have had with the Merlin — one of your impudent forebears, no doubt — I can see I will have with you, sir. Yet it is for the bluntness of your counsel, which is more use to me than sweet words, that I have chosen you, rather than another, to carry out a task for me.' She looked at Nimue, and her gaunt face softened a little.

'Your wife has long been known to us in her own right as her father's daughter, and esteemed for her own particular virtues. As your lady she is doubly valuable to us. She will travel with you and thus dispel suspicion as to your true purpose.'

Pendragon's dark brows shifted.

'You will go to France, to Paris,' Elizabeth ordered preremptorily. 'And elsewhere if you must. You will answer only to me, and carry out my instructions in private. You will seek out this man, this Nicolas Flamel — or his wife, if either live, as has been reported. Or else you will bring me some evidence that both of them are in their grave and rotting. I command you as your Queen. And I — .' She paused.

'I ask you as an old woman, who would know, for the quiet of my own mind, whether death is the end.'

Nimue could not help herself. She turned to her husband, her eyes eloquent. Pendragon was still, unmoving, then he smiled, the scars on his face unable in their harshness to disguise the light that softened his eyes.

'Madam, you will never be old. And as for death, you have said yourself that you met and vanquished him years since. So must all do who would live, whether in this world or the next.'

Elizabeth tapped her foot, most amazingly appearing at a loss. Then she threw a half-hearted barb in Nimue's direction.

'Is there some philtre by means of which you can curb your wizard's forward tongue, lady? For sure, this man has no need of spells, his voice can make his preaching subtle and sinful as sweet music, though he speaks only and does not sing. God's blood, if I had been younger — . You might have earned my displeasure for marrying with such a one, when he might have — . Hmm.' She continued to stare thoughtfully at Pendragon, who smiled.

'If Your Grace had been present when we met, my lord would never have looked twice at me,' Nimue felt herself saying very prettily, and Elizabeth, pleased at her flattering outrageousness, chose to abandon the game and all pretence. She threw back her head and laughed, then, leaning forward, pinched Nimue's cheek so that it stung.

'Ha! Have I lost my 'other Welsh wizard' Gwynne, only to have two more to plague me? Your father, too could always win at fair words, child, though he always spoke true. Well, you have earned each other. And because I will reveal my thoughts on this matter to no-one else, you will be my eyes and go for me to France.' She pursed her lips. 'Death holds nothing with which to threaten me, for I have seen it already. But my people, the women who clutch their stomachs to give birth, and die in their own blood, hardly out of their own babyhood — shall there not be life for them? And an easy passing for those whose life is pain? You are familiar with thoughts such as these. I am a temporal ruler, I cannot charge the waves and the shadows. Yet, if there is a way — .'

'Such power, unwisely used, madam, could let loose the fiends of hell,' Pendragon said uncompromisingly, and Nimue protested before she could help herself.

'It is true, yet you taught me otherwise, my dear lord. As with water — as with gold — . It is not the element that is evil, but the misuse of it. And if there could be an end to suffering — to the fear of the grave — .'

She waited, and the Queen too was silent.

Much needed to be spoken of. Ruffard Rowland and Owain ab Owain in Wales, were safeguarding the future of Pendragon tower, the land and the people who looked to their lord. Within the earth, the gold still waited. The ruined, blackened stones must be rebuilt. And Nimue's house, the Queen's gift, where her people were even now busily about their daily tasks, stood gracious and stately behind its high walls, beside the Thames.

* * *

At last, Pendragon made his reverence to the Queen and, turning to Nimue, took both her hands.

'We will go,' he said, very low. 'The land will still be there when we return, and Owain guards it well. We will go together, you and I, and I will honour my pledge to you, witch, as my lady and my wife. Though Pendragon has burned and I cannot spread my mother's quilt for you nor light the candles to welcome you to my tower — .' He smiled down into her eyes. 'We will find another tower and drink together from the loving cup and celebrate our wedding night. And together, we will greet the dawn.'

THE END